ABOUT THIS BOOK

Welcome to Havenwood Falls, home to sexy men, strong women, and neighbors who bite. Discover supernatural mystery, thrills, and romance in a place where everyone has a deep, dark, and often deadly secret. This is only but one...

It takes the fallen to save the damned.

Harper Sinclair doesn't own any books. If she can avoid it, she doesn't read or write at all. Words are dangerous. Beyond the cover of a book, words rearrange themselves for Harper, becoming messages from beyond. Brutal messages. Terrible messages. When she writes, awful things flow from her fingers. She's a spiritual writer haunted by demons.

Lucas Fox is one of the fallen, an angel whose murderous past keeps him from Heaven, and whose protective, chivalrous nature keeps him from Hell. He lives between worlds, content to enjoy his vices while doing just enough to keep him out of the underworld.

But when Harper is forced to sign a contract for a house she buys in Havenwood Falls, the words that appear aren't her name. Instead, she pens a dire message threatening a fallen angel whose old alliance with a ruler of Hell has made him the target of a powerful demon lord. A warning that draws Lucas Fox to Havenwood Falls to settle old scores and puts Harper Sinclair directly in the line of danger.

INK & FIRE

A HAVENWOOD FALLS NOVELLA

R.K. RYALS

HAVENWOOD FALLS BOOKS

Forget You Not by Kristie Cook

Old Wounds by Susan Burdorf

Fate, Love & Loyalty by E.J. Fechenda

The Winged & the Wicked by T.V. Hahn & Kristie Cook

Alpha's Queen by Lila Felix

Ink & Fire by R.K. Ryals

Lose You Not by Kristie Cook

Tragic Ink by Heather Hildenbrand

Nowhere to Hide by Belinda Boring

Flames Among the Frost by Amy Hale

Rock Me Gently by Susan Burdorf

From the Embers by Amy Miles

Defying Gravity by Kallie Ross

Break Me Not by Kristie Cook

How the Dead Lie by Stacey Rourke

The Lurkers Within by Danielle Bannister

The Collector: Awakening by Kristie Cook, R.K. Ryals, Belinda Boring & Nadirah Foxx

Addicted to You by Belinda Boring

Affliction Mine by C.J. Pinard

The Ward & the Wanderers by T.V. Hahn

Toil & Trouble by Melissa Wright

Of Salt and Stars by Seven Jane

Redefined by Morgan Wylie

Betrayal Among the Frost by Amy Hale

Forever Loyal by E.J. Fechenda

Fate's Demand by Emily Cyr

The Wu & the Wand by T.V. Hahn

A Demon's Redemption by JD Nelson

Also try the YA line, Havenwood Falls High; the historical paranormal line, Legends of Havenwood Falls; the darker, sexier side of town, Havenwood Falls Sin & Silk; and the local supernatural college, Sun & Moon Academy.

Stay up to date at www.HavenwoodFalls.com

OTHER BOOKS BY R.K. RYALS

The Redemption Series

Redemption

Ransom

Retribution

Revelation

The Acropolis Series

The Acropolis

The Labyrinth

Deliverance

The Thorne Trilogy

Cursed

Possessed

Dancing with the Devil

In the Land of Tea and Ravens (Standalone book)

The Scribes of Medeisia Series

Mark of the Mage

Tempest

Fist of the Furor

City in Ruins

The Standalone Embrace Yourself Series

The Story of Awkward

An Introvert's Tale

The Singing River

For those who know the power behind words.

Words are mighty warriors that can shake mountains even when whispered.

By that sin fell the angels.
—William Shakespeare

PROLOGUE

*D*anger rises in the darkness. Shadows weave in and out of nothingness, the Infernum a screaming mess of imagined pain, for the fear of pain is often much worse than the actual hurt.

Distorted, faceless creatures march through an empty space filled with evil intentions. Trapped, they beg for mercy.

In the midst of chaos, a man's face appears, as beguiling as it is dreadful. Hair the color of midnight, dark eyes touched with crimson, and a hard face lined with smoke and madness stares into emptiness.

The Infernum swallows its prisoners whole.

But not for long. Not for one of them.

"The time has come." Lips curl in a sickening smile, a forked tongue darting out to taste the air.

CHAPTER 1

*M*y aunt once told me that anything I ever needed to know about life I could find in a Van Morrison song. Apparently, she'd experienced all of her firsts to his music: first date, first kiss, and her first time losing her virginity. I say first because my aunt is continually losing her virginity. Something about taking it back and starting over every time she feels let down by an experience. At forty-eight years old and after a recent less-than-satisfying encounter, Eloise Sinclair is now a virgin again.

Hanging turquoise beads *click click* together as Eloise exits the back of her new age shop Into the Mystic, cradling a steaming mug, the contents smelling suspiciously of mugwort and bourbon. The mugwort is for enhancing her psychic abilities. The bourbon is for her nerves.

A long-sleeved purple tunic swings against polka-dotted leggings as she approaches me, wisps of auburn hair falling into perceptive brown eyes. "The Pen Is Mightier Than the Sword."

She raises her mug at me. The Van Morrison song title is all it takes. I've heard way too much of my aunt's music playlist. She's relating my life to the song.

"Do your clients enjoy translating Morrisonese, or is this just for my benefit?" I grimace at the song choice. "Wrong one for me."

"You assume."

"If this is about the meeting I have at the plaza this afternoon—"

"It's about your fate," Eloise cuts me off cryptically.

My family makes deals with destiny, usually other people's. It pays the rent and the utility bills. The mugwort and the bourbon, too. For prices ranging anywhere from one hundred to three hundred dollars an hour—all depending on the type of reading—my aunt Eloise can discern a client's future, past, or present.

She is psychic. I am, too. Only, my abilities come with a curse. A rather inconvenient one.

Eloise studies me over the rim of her mug, her gaze raking over my loose brown hair and makeup-less green eyes before dropping to my solid navy sweatshirt and skinny jeans. "You couldn't have tried a little harder for such a momentous occasion?"

I glance down at myself. "For picking up a set of keys?"

"Hmm."

My gaze roams over the shop, careful not to linger on anything too long. This shop and the basement apartment downstairs are home. For the last twenty-three years, it has been everything. The purple walls, the brightly painted bookshelves stocked with new age books, the scarf-covered tables littered with candles, the glass cases full of jewelry and crystals, the mauve and gold chaise lounge, the stuffed blue-checked chairs, the herbal tea counter, and the beaded curtains leading to the basement stairs and the back of the shop all wail at me. Memories have a way of making inanimate objects speak.

Or maybe I am just super emotional.

"Did you 'hmm' at me?" I ask, following Aunt Eloise to the front door.

She flips over the open sign, arches a brow, and hmms again.

Outside, the morning sun sweeps like spilled pastel paints down Eleventh Street, the rays turning the light dusting of snow on the shop rooftops on the other side of the square into glitter. The sun brings the stores—Backwoods Sport & Ski, Howe's Herbal Shoppe, and Tragic Ink—to life. Like a necromancer raising the dead. Darkness touched by light.

I have a lot of experience with darkness, with beasts, and with life. That's what happens when your psychic abilities are tied to evil.

Eloise calls what she does spiritually guiding people's lives.

I sentence them to damnation.

Spiritual writing, my aunt calls it. Communication from the dead translated through written words. It all sounds so harmless.

I was barely old enough to write when I scribed my first message. Wide-eyed and excited, I handed the note to a man in town, the words *u will die and deemuns will feest on ur sol* scrawled in crayon. As if this was a completely normal thing for a gap-toothed five-year-old girl to do. As if I was delivering a winning lottery ticket rather than a death sentence.

Turns out, people don't like knowing when they're going to die. They like even less knowing their souls are indulgent treats for demons.

The man cried. I didn't come out of my room for two days.

Worse yet, he was a mortal, and he *died*.

That night, the Court of the Sun and the Moon came for me, everyone solemn-faced and full of regret. A world of secrets was revealed —secrets about the town I lived in and the people I loved. Havenwood Falls, Colorado, is a sanctuary for people and creatures with supernatural abilities. It's also home to mortals. Oh, and ironically, demons, but not the kind of demons that like me. Not the soul-sucking terrible horrible creatures that I seem to channel.

The rules of our town are simple: protect the secret and don't kill the mortals.

At five years old, I was off to a bad start.

My aunt pats me on the cheek, breaking me out of my thoughts, her hand warm from the mug. "Hmm."

Nothing good ever comes from Eloise's hmms.

Snatching her mug, I gulp down the mugwort and bourbon. For the nerves, not the mental enhancement.

"It's a house," I say. Not just any house. *My* house. My first house. A place all my own, completely book- and writing-free. That's a lot more difficult than it sounds.

Words are everywhere. On television, clothes, signs, groceries, phones . . . the list goes on forever. I've trained myself to look at things without actually *looking* at them. If it's possible to avoid my "gift," then I do it.

The bell at the front of the store *dings*.

"You're not going to want the chamomile or candles," Eloise says from behind one of the displays. She doesn't have to see the customer to know why she's come. "It's oolong tea and a charged black tourmaline crystal for you. Trust me. You have all kinds of negative energy attached to you, and it is not good for your health."

At least her gift doesn't kill people.

I'm still stuck on Eloise's hmms.

The hmms chase me through the rest of the morning and through the streets of Havenwood Falls. It's too early for my meeting at the plaza when I leave my aunt's shop, so I am in no hurry when I hit Main Street on foot, my hands tucked deep within my coat pockets. I have a bad habit of facing my weaknesses while also avoiding them. This is why I find myself standing in front of Shelf Indulgence, a bookstore on Main Street, the smell of coffee wafting from Coffee Haven next door.

My eyes drift over the large showcase window so quickly that everything inside is merely a blur, before my gaze falls to my feet, puffs of air the only thing between me and the ground. Shelf Indulgence is my own personal hell. A place full of everything I wish I could touch and see. A place full of everything I wish I could *be*. The owner, a witch named Sedona Mathews, always decorates the showcase window with wildly creative displays. I'm both tempted and afraid to look at it. I am blind without being blind, my mind used to counting steps and knowing exactly where everything is, so that I can avoid anything new and potentially dangerous. My mind hates change, but my heart craves it.

"Harper?" a familiar female voice calls.

A pair of small brown boots settle next to mine on the sidewalk, and I let my gaze slide up them, over Thanksgiving-themed leggings and a long burgundy tunic to a pale face surrounded by silvery blond hair. Her skin positively glows. Concerned turquoise eyes stare at me. Willow Fairchild, the owner of Coffee Haven, and as of a few months ago, a new mother. Motherhood agrees with her.

She smiles. "It's been a few days since I saw you down this way. Do you have any new photographs for me? Your last set was popular with the customers."

I try to talk and can't, my words caught somewhere between the emotions building within me and the desire to walk inside Coffee Haven to see the new artwork Willow has displayed.

Silence stretches between us.

Reaching out, Willow squeezes my shoulder gently. "You let me know when you do, okay?" Profound understanding colors her eyes a deeper shade of turquoise, and I know she senses my unease and troubled thoughts. Willow, like many of the town's residents, is a supernatural, an empathetic fae with the power to sense emotions.

Throwing me a final smile, she enters Coffee Haven. A blast of warm air and the smell of blueberry scones hits me. I inhale, sucking in the scent and the warm feeling that comes with it.

Cars and pedestrians meander slowly around my spot on the sidewalk, and I turn away from the bookstore and coffee shop, my gaze settling on the town square across the street and a sparkling fountain in the distance. A work truck is parked near the curb, and a man leans against it, a cup of coffee cradled in his hands. Like with most of the locals, I've seen him before, but I don't know him. I'm not a social person, even though I think I could be if things were different.

This man is broad, a beard protecting his face from the cold, and he sips the coffee, watching me. When my eyes catch his, he pauses, dips his head, and lifts his cup. There are secrets lurking in his gaze, and even though it's unnerving to find him observing me, I don't feel threatened. I have a strange feeling he's studying me for the same reason I study him back. Secrets. There are secrets everywhere in this town.

Today, however, secrets are the least of my concerns. Today, I'm making Harper history. Giddy excitement fills me, the emotions overwhelming everything else, and I slip down the street. Away from the stranger. Away from Shelf Indulgence and my wishes. Away from Willow Fairchild and her empathetic understanding.

Away from everything I know and toward something new.

CHAPTER 2

The minute I walk into the Turner Real Estate office, I know I'm in trouble.

There isn't much to the small space. Part of Miller's Plaza on the west side of town and right off of the street, it is basically a king-sized cubicle. A large desk rests against the back wall with two burgundy-cushioned chairs positioned before it and bookshelves flanking it. An area rug is thrown over old wooden floors, and a small hallway off to the side leads to whatever is kept in the back.

It's not the office that bothers me. It's the stack of papers fanned out across the desk.

I let my gaze slide quickly over the pages before dropping it to the floor.

Jeanine Turner, a tall, slender, raven-haired woman, greets me at the door, her smile a little too perky, her eyes way too sharp.

"Today is your day, Harper Sinclair!" She high-fives the air. "I just have one place we missed in the paperwork the other day that I need you to sign. Nothing serious. It's mainly for my own personal records."

My mouth turns to sawdust. "My aunt takes care of my paperwork."

Jeanine waves away my words. "It's one signature. We got the legal stuff in closing. This is for my records. I don't know if the pages stuck together or if Eloise overlooked it. You can sign your name, can't you?"

Her condescending tone stiffens my spine. I'm not illiterate, and she knows it. What she doesn't know is what's actually wrong with me. Because Jeanine is mortal, I'm not at liberty to discuss my demon-possessed writing skills.

Jeanine slides behind her desk, steeples her fingers, and says, "We can wait on your aunt, but I leave for vacation in," she checks a clock on the wall, "ten minutes."

I don't check the time. Even though my abilities don't seem to include a problem with numbers, I only look at them when absolutely necessary, and usually only long enough to keep track of the day.

As for Jeanine, she's lying. I can smell it on her, and I'm not even a shifter. Technically, I am just as human as she is. Just with extrasensory abilities.

This is what I get for using a mortal agency. The Court has ways of working around my issues, which is why I'm still in Havenwood Falls. I can't risk leaving.

I start to sit in one of the cushy chairs, and then decide against it. "I need this done now."

I *want* this done now.

"Then I suggest you sign on the dotted line. I'd hate to hold the keys on a technicality."

I make my living as a nature photographer. Vintage cameras. Old film. Hours spent inside a darkroom. Days spent hiking in the mountains. Jeanine reminds me of a buzzard, a scavenger reeking of decay. I'm the roadkill.

For business and financial matters, I gave power of attorney to my aunt, but I'm legally able to sign if necessary.

I don't want to wait a week to move into my home, and because I'm terrible with confrontation, I don't call her bluff on the vacation. Honestly, I *don't want* to call her bluff. I want this home in every sense of the word. I want it to be mine. Something with my actual signature on it. Not my aunt's or someone's from the Court. *Mine.*

Sitting, I lock gazes with Jeanine. "I need a pen."

The ballpoint she hands me feels foreign and heavy in my fingers.

Jeanine slides a sheet of paper in front of me, the signature line clearly marked by a red sticky flag. Words dance, and I try not to look at them, my gaze focused on the tab. It's the color of blood.

I set the pen against the paper.

The world falls apart.

Dark energy rushes me, overwhelmingly tragic, the power turning my fingers into monsters. Words whisper through my head. Dreadful words. *Death. Blood. Mine.* I am a prisoner to the pain and the agony. The demons howl, each of them begging me to channel them.

If I could fall to my knees and beg them to stop, I would. A tear slips down my cheek, and I fight, sweat beading up along my brow as I try to drop the pen. Not fighting feels like giving up.

"Please," I whimper.

"Write it!" One voice is more persistent than the rest. My hand spasms, the world going black. The way it always does.

Jeanine Turner screams.

When I come to, my hand remains poised over the paper, the ballpoint pen having left a line of frantically scrawled words. *You will have a place in Hell, Lucas Fox. Cast and chained in the Infernum of darkness. Death to the messenger. Death to those who give her sanctuary.*

I inhale . . . or try to.

An invisible vise grips me by the neck, cutting off my oxygen supply, and I claw at my skin desperately. It makes no difference. I belong to a world of darkness.

With little effort, the spirit attached to me lifts me off the chair and throws me across the room.

My head slams against the office's glass entrance, my vision blurring. Adrenaline and fear pump through my system, dulling the pain. People move on the sidewalk beyond, and I panic even while gasping for air. I can't let anyone see me like this. First rule of thumb: protect the humans.

Still struggling to breathe, I crawl back across the room, a trail of blood dripping behind me. Jeanine's screams rise, shrill and deafening, the sound a jackhammer in my head.

The Court is going to kill me.

My knees and hands dig into the wooden floor, my heart racing as I lurch into the back hallway. Two doorways greet me, and I propel myself through the closest one, my body landing on a tiled bathroom floor. Slamming the door, I lock it.

The demon relinquishes me, and I drag in air through my lungs, his words etched into my brain. *Death to the messenger. Death to those who give her sanctuary.*

Death simply because I wanted something to call mine. Death simply because I wanted to be able to write my own name.

Tears mingle with blood on the floor beneath me. Red on black on white. The story of my life.

CHAPTER 3

"*H*arper?"

My aunt's voice is like a balm on an open wound, and even though I want nothing more than to throw open the bathroom door and run into her arms, I don't. I remain in a fetal position, my cheek pressed against a floor I hope has been cleaned in the last week. It's too potpourri-y in here, which is never good. No one uses potpourri this strong unless they're trying to hide something. Mold. Urine. Germs.

"Harper," my aunt tries again.

"It's bad this time," I tell her, my gaze on the crack under the door. She's wearing tennis shoes, which means this is serious. Aunt Eloise owns one pair of tennis shoes—a pair of neon yellow Velcro monstrosities—and she only wears them when there's an emergency and she's in a hurry. Otherwise, she dons outrageously colored boots or ballet flats. The bright tennis shoes look like caution tape and rightly so.

Jeanine Turner yells something unintelligible from her office.

Aunt Eloise answers her with, "It's fine. Everything's okay. She just has a thing for bathrooms." She raps on the door. "Harper, honey, you've got to open up. You're scaring the mortal."

I glare at her feet. "This is why you were 'hmming' at me earlier, isn't it? You knew!"

"She flew across the room!" Jeanine roars, her voice rising. "Explain that!"

"Addie, why don't you take Mrs. Turner out for some fresh air?" another voice breaks in.

I would know that voice anywhere. Saundra Beaumont. A powerful witch of one of the founding families of the Luna Coven. She also serves on the Court of the Sun and the Moon, a court that basically runs Havenwood Falls. All of the members are from old blood and old money.

"I didn't mean to," I immediately defend.

A pair of navy high heels joins Eloise's worn sneakers. Old family blood versus us.

"Calm yourself, Harper," Saundra says firmly. "We can fix what happened here." Papers rustle, and I cringe. "As for what you wrote, that's another story."

"I'm sorry." Apologizing is habit for me. I've been practicing the art of apology ever since I first entered the Court of the Sun and the Moon. Then, I had been an awestruck child standing in a windowless room in the City Hall's basement, candlelight flickering off of sympathetic faces.

Oh, how I have fallen.

The message I wrote at five years old isn't the only message I've scribed. I did learn how to read and write, after all. Not to mention it's hard to completely avoid words, especially as a child, but the Court has steadily protected me and the people I inadvertently threatened while I learned to be what I am now: detached from the world. As far as I know, I've only caused one death with my curse.

"I just want the keys to my house," I say weakly. No potpourri for my bathroom. I will scrub my toilets.

"Come out," Saundra soothes. "Get medical attention. Go home with your aunt. What's happening to you is wrong, Harper. No one should have to see their family . . ." She pauses, and I know she's looking at my aunt. When her voice comes again, it's closer to the floor, surprising me. I'm having a hard time imagining the silver-haired, suit-wearing woman stooping. "Generational curses be damned. We protect the supes and the mortals, Harper. We made a promise to you and to your aunt. You can't help what's happening to you."

"He's coming," I whisper. From the paper she's holding, she knows who I mean.

"We'll have someone stronger here to meet him."

Finally sitting up, I reach over and flip the lock on the door. My aunt opens it, her concerned gaze finding my face. She looks every bit the eccentric with her colorful clothes, tennis shoes, and hoop earrings. Saundra is her opposite in every way.

I stare up at them. "I still want the keys to my house."

Arching a brow, Saundra lifts her hand, a set of keys dangling from her fingers.

Taking them, Eloise leans down next to me and presses them into my hand. "I didn't know this would happen. I saw something big, but not this . . . darkness." She starts to hug me, and then stops. I don't do hugs. "Let's get you cleaned up. The Court will take care of the rest."

Amnesia spells. Wards. Secrets. The Court of the Sun and the Moon runs this town on magic and mystery.

"My soul hurts," I breathe.

"Oh, honey, I know." She smooths a hand over my blood-dampened hair, and murmurs, "Harpists harp harping. Angels airily dancing. On clouds, casting glances. Their eyes glowing brightly. Guarding. Guiding. And that's how I got my name. Or so my mother says."

"No Van Morrison right now."

"It's not Van Morrison," Eloise reveals. "Your mother wrote that."

"Really?" Even if she's lying, it's a good distraction.

"Really. Right before she died, she took your dad's hand and said, 'Name her Harper.' We figured it was an omen. They say people see things right before they die."

I killed her, too, I think.

Eloise helps me to my feet, throws a coat around my shoulders, pulls a hoodie up over my head, and leads me out a back door at the end of the hall. Past witches I don't stop to talk to and a dazed Jeanine Turner. She won't remember this tomorrow. Quite possibly, she won't even remember her vacation.

I fist my hand around the keys until the metal bites into my flesh.

THAT NIGHT, after hours of forced wakefulness, I fall into a deep, exhausted sleep, my sore body curled around a pillow, blankets wrapping me, and my aunt's familiar apartment surrounding me.

Then, I dream.

. . .

NIGHT SWALLOWS THE DAYLIGHT.

I am standing on a mountain, a brisk wind lifting my hair against my face. There's snow on the air, the smell of it heavy and thick.

A full moon shines down on a silver world, on a sleepy town full of people I've known forever. Streets, shops, parks, and cemeteries I could walk in my sleep spread out like pieces on a board game.

My town. No road map. No signs.

Words are dangerous, so I navigate without them. My mind is an atlas of landmarks. Over two miles of stamped images: avenues named after the Old Families, a town square, a park with a lake, a ski resort, a myriad of residences ranging in income and style, and mountain trails. Housing developments dot the town: Havenwood Heights, Creekwood, Havenstone, and Havenwood Village. Shops I rarely visit out of fear stare up at me: Howe's Herbal Shoppe, Soothing Sips, Coffee Haven, Callie's Consignments, Shelf Indulgence, and Tragic Ink among many.

In the mountains are other things—Cooley Creek, Mathews River, Smalls Falls, Peacock Lake, Bels Creek, Hale Creek—beautiful landmarks I've made a living hiking so that I can capture the animals and flora on film, being careful not to snap pictures of the shifters and other supernatural creatures that prowl the trails with me.

Somewhere in the forest, a wolf howls.

"It's a beautiful town," a gravelly voice says, the words a part of the wind. "What a shame it would be if I destroyed it."

"Why would you destroy it?" My words sound far away, as if I'm floating outside of my body instead of inhabiting it.

"Because I can." Evil doesn't always need a reason to do things. "Can't you see the future, psychic?"

Above me, the moon turns red. Something wet and sticky drips on my face, and I swipe at it, horrified when my hand comes away covered in a substance that looks suspiciously like blood.

Black shadows so dark even the night can't hide them drop out of the sky, descending on the town. Screams rise from the streets below. Agonizing screams.

"They're dying," the voice gloats. "They're all dying."

"No!"

From the edge of the woods, animals emerge. They crawl toward me, all *of them wounded, blood spilling out of their sides. Shifters. All of them are shifters. Shifters I know. People I spend every day passing on the streets. People I talk to. Friends.*

"*Help us,*" *they beg.*

Blood. There's so much blood.

The shifters crawl closer, reaching, their prone figures so close I can see the agony etched into their faces.

"*No!*" *I scream.*

Closing my eyes, I cover my ears and fall to my knees.

Only, I don't hit the ground. My knees land on air, and I am falling, falling, falling.

WHEN I COME TO, I stare into a dark room touched by a night-light that's been in my aunt's apartment for as long as I can remember. It's shaped like a star, and I used to make wishes on it. *Star light, star bright, first star I see tonight.*

That was before I learned wishes are scary things. That was before I learned it is much easier to wish for something than it is to make it happen.

CHAPTER 4

*L*ight finger-shaped bruises form around my neck, and I spend the next few days pulling the collar of my coat up, my hair swinging loose. Other than the bruising and a mild concussion, the worst thing I suffer is a blow to my pride. Nothing yells adulting quite like being found in a fetal position on the bathroom floor covered in blood and shame.

After three days of sweat-inducing terrifying nightmares—the same one every night—sympathetic stares, Court interrogations, and my aunt's outrageous herbal concoctions, relief washes over me the minute I step into the driveway of my new home. It's perfect. A remote, fully furnished, one-bedroom log cabin in the mountains, the home is everything I had worked to achieve: independence.

Inhaling the cold mountain air, I sling a camera bag over my shoulder before tugging the single rolling suitcase after me. My life in one bag and one suitcase. I don't know if that's sad or impressive.

Mine.

My fingers tremble when I insert the key in the lock, the sound of it clicking open like fireworks on the Fourth of July.

Now would be a good time for intro music, something about freedom and home, but all I get is the heavy arched door creaking open on its iron hinges. The door is part of the reason I love the place. Sunlight spills in like a spotlight on stage, revealing a stuffed leather sofa, wood-burning fireplace, and stone-accented kitchen, but the best part is what the place is missing.

No television. No books. No cell phones. No signs.

No trouble.

You will have a place in Hell, Lucas Fox. Cast and chained in the Infernum of darkness. Death to the messenger. Death to those who give her sanctuary.

The message haunts me, but I push it away. I'm sick of evil controlling my life.

Setting the suitcase and camera bag inside the entry, I switch on the lights and quietly shut the door behind me, my fingers running over the frame. *Home.* Excitement burrows a den in my heart.

Unable to stop smiling, I move through the house doing mundane things I never thought I'd appreciate: starting a fire, unpacking clothes, and sweeping the floors with a broom I find in the hallway utility closet.

My fireplace. My dust. My broom.

In the middle of my living room, I take it all in, embarrassed by the tears pricking the back of my eyes. I am proud of this.

"They tell me you're the messenger," a low voice says from the direction of the kitchen.

I freeze, goosebumps rising on my skin, my fingers gripping the broom in my hand so hard my knuckles turn a mottled shade of red, the flesh around it pallid.

Death to the messenger.

Chest heaving, I turn slowly.

A man—no, a golden *Adonis*—leans against the island bar separating the kitchen from the living area. He's tall, over six feet, with blond hair cropped close to his head and eyes so blue, it's like looking at the sky. Jeans rest low on his hips, and a white button-up shirt hugs a muscular frame too magnificent to be covered up.

He's too *everything* to be human, *and* he came out of nowhere. This should be what frightens me the most, but sadly, I'm used to strange things happening to me. Or, more accurately, me *doing* strange things. Like me relaying demonic words and images I shouldn't see or me being hurled across an office by an evil entity. This, however, would be the first time an actual man appeared.

Considering my gifts, he can be only one thing.

I wield the broom like a sword. "I don't know what you are or what you want, but know that I won't go down without putting up one hell of a fight."

He studies me, his gaze flicking over the bruises on my neck before falling to the broom. "Congratulations, Ms. Sinclair. I've got to say, this is the first time I've ever been challenged with a broom." Pushing away from the bar, he steps toward me.

I stumble backward. He knows my name.

"I'm not here to harm you," he promises.

Jabbing the air with my makeshift weapon, I circle toward the front door and then stop, because I refuse to leave my house. "Prove it. Keep your distance." He pauses, and I swallow tears. There's nothing worse than feeling the urge to cry when angry. "Why won't all of you leave me alone? You can't let me have even this? Stealing words from me wasn't enough? Taking away a normal life wasn't enough?"

His chin rises, and I can't help but notice how sharp his face is. He's more rugged than beautiful. Terrifying even.

"I'm not a demon," he reveals.

My grip on the broom loosens and then tightens again. "You're lying. You can't be anything else. Only demons and evil spirits come to me."

"They come to you in messages. Do I look like a message to you?" he asks.

"Do the bruises on my neck look like a message?"

"Quite frankly, yes."

The broom wavers. "What are you?"

He smirks. "More like *who* am I? You should know. You channeled the asshole who threatened me."

You will have a place in Hell, Lucas Fox. Cast and chained in the Infernum of darkness. Death to the messenger. Death to those who give her sanctuary.

The broom hits the floor. "Lucas Fox."

"I never did understand the mortal need for last names."

He's moved closer while speaking, and I keep backing away, circling so that I'm not caught against a wall.

"Heritage. Family," I reply, unsure why I care. At one point, I have to climb on the arm of my new couch.

Lucas's eyes twinkle. "They didn't tell me you were so young . . . or so intriguing."

"Who are they?"

"The Court. Your town's Court. You know, the whole Sun and Moon thing?"

Startled, I almost fall off the sofa, my fingers finding purchase on the leather. "The Court sent you?"

Lucas stops in front of the couch, and I drop down behind it, the sofa a shield between us.

"They would have told me." I glance around frantically. "S-supernatural newcomers are supposed to register with the Court. The wards . . . they'll know you're here." I shake a finger at him. "Demons aren't immune."

He smiles. "They summoned me with quite an interesting message. I told you I'm not a demon, and I'm not very good with rules. They'll know I'm here when I'm ready for them to know. Going to them first would have been a lot less interesting than this." Glancing at the floor, he cocks a brow. "I kind of miss the broom. You looked cute with it."

What dignity I have left bristles at his comment. "You've got a lot of . . ." The words trail off, my eyes widening. Only one kind of supernatural being is immune to the Court and the wards, and as far as I know, not many of them make their homes in Havenwood Falls. "You're an angel." Shock colors my words.

He dips his head. "Well done, Harper." Spreading his arms wide, he adds, "Now that we've gotten that out of the way, do you want to tell me why I smell Hell on you?"

I may not watch television or read any books, but I do listen to a lot of audiobooks on CDs from which my aunt removes the labels. Mostly science fiction and romance, because sci-fi is cool and romance is, well, romance.

The last thing a girl ever wants to hear from anyone—it doesn't matter who it is—is that they smell like Hell.

It takes everything I've got not to sniff myself. "Hell has a smell?"

He laughs, the sound masculine and deep. It gives me an odd feeling, as if it's the kind of laugh that gives purpose to life, which seems weird, and yet . . . maybe not. Every time I've accidentally channeled a demon over the years, it felt like something was stolen from me. This laugh—an *angel's* laugh—gives something back.

For a woman drowning in darkness, it's a heady feeling.

"It doesn't smell like mortals would assume," Lucas assures me. "It's not all brimstone and sulfur." His eyes shine. "It smells like sin."

"Which is bad, right?"

"To some." The way he arches his brows suggests he isn't one of the "some."

My mouth gapes. "You're fallen." The words come out on a whisper. It doesn't take much to figure out what he is. Lucas has that *how can something that looks so good be so bad* feel to him, and he definitely doesn't smell like Hell.

He sits on the arm of the couch, and I'm tempted to lunge for my broom. Fallen angels have to be fallen for a reason, right?

"Don't look so horrified," he says. "Considering the evil you channeled, you're going to be glad I am who I am. I feel him. He shouldn't be coming, but he is. You and this town are going to need me."

His warning makes my heart race, and I touch the bruises on my neck. "If he's a demon—"

"He's more than a demon. He's an archdemon. A lord of Hell. A part of the highest order in the underworld. You called royalty, Ms. Sinclair."

I am pretty sure I've forgotten how to breathe.

Lucas stands. "You have a nice home."

A thank you hangs off the tip of my tongue, but it never makes it out of my mouth before Lucas suddenly vanishes.

My legs give out, and I sink to the floor, the fire crackling in the hearth the only sound in the room. The blaze should warm me, but I feel cold. *Way* too cold.

Fallen angels. Archdemons.

I own a house. I don't know why I cling to that thought. Maybe because, with everything happening to me, I need a reminder that a little piece of me remains.

There's only one remedy for the sick feeling in my stomach: grilled cheese sandwiches.

That's the thing with issues like mine. After years of having to face the monsters under my bed, or in my case, out of accidental messages, I've had to find ways to cope. Wine is a pretty good remedy. Hell, there've been times I've just thrown back the hard stuff, but drunkenness means losing control. Losing control means forgetting not to read messages or write. That leaves food. Forget ice cream. There's nothing better for stress eating than carbs and melted cheese. And butter.

Oh, the butter.

CHAPTER 5

*B*arely twenty-four hours into living on my own, and I'm back in town, the sun shining down on my uncovered head, my coat pulled tightly closed. Despite growing up in the mountains, I am always cold, which is the reason I have a tendency to tuck insole foot warmers into the bottom of my boots and hand warmers into the pockets of my coat. If I can keep my feet warm, the rest of me manages.

Pedestrians crowd the sidewalk despite the late November temperatures, most of them taking advantage of the Thanksgiving week sales. Murmurs of conversation ride the wind, puffed breaths mingling with the smells of coffee and food.

I pause outside my aunt's shop, the words Into the Mystic New Age Books and Gifts burned into a wooden sign hanging above my head. I don't look up at it. My breath leaves condensation on the store's glass door, the heat clouding the interior.

My stomach hurts. Anxiety, maybe? Or the ridiculous amount of greasy grilled cheese sandwiches I inhaled the night before.

The bell dings when I enter. "Aunt Eloise," I call, "we need to talk."

Beads clink together. "What do you think about reserving an area of the park for storytellers at the psychic fair this year? Maybe dressed as authentic minstrels?" In white tights and a top covered in swirly colors, my aunt looks like a lollipop. A lollipop that's avoiding eye contact. "Imagine how enthralling and vivid it would be."

Every year on the spring equinox, Eloise runs an Into the Mystic

New Age and Psychic Fair in Town Square Park. She starts planning the next year's event as soon as the current one ends, and as much as I love helping her come up with ideas, I know a distraction when I see one.

"The Court sent me an angel. A *fallen* angel." The statement sits in the air between us, heavy and accusing.

Eloise tugs on one of her hoop earrings. She has eight earrings in all, most of them studs and none of them the same color. "I know. Saundra informed me." She tugs harder on the hoop. "Technically, they sent you the angel your message called out by name."

"Hmm." It feels good to throw out a few hmms of my own, instead of receiving them.

"He's a warrior," Eloise tries again. "There aren't many high-ranking supernaturals who don't know who Lucas Fox is."

"Hmm." My arms cross.

"He fell from the highest order an angel can fall from. He's one of the most powerful of his kind. That's all I know, Harper."

"Is he dangerous?" I ask, dropping my arms. "Because he just showed up at my house. Out of nowhere."

Moving past me to the table she keeps stocked with candles, she begins sorting them. First by size and then by color. "The Court wouldn't bring in someone dangerous."

"That's a lie," I snap, surprising us both. "I'm dangerous, and they let me live here."

"Harper—"

"Is he dangerous to *me*?"

I leave what I really want to ask unsaid. She knows. Because of my curse, I should have never taken the pen. I should have never attempted to write my name. I not only put people in danger, I put the entire town at risk. The Court has every right to punish me.

A sudden brilliant light fills the room, followed by a familiar golden visage. "Give me a little credit, sweetheart. I don't punish people unless I have a personal reason to."

Eloise knocks over two of her candles. I nearly fall into a display of essential oils.

"I expected a little fanfare, but nearly fainting . . . I'm humbled." Lucas Fox saunters across the shop, his blue eyes glinting.

Eloise rights the candles. "I had heard you were arrogant."

He smiles. "I had heard you were charming."

"I haven't heard anything." Frustration turns my voice into a growl. "And that light thing," I wave at Lucas, "you couldn't have done that when we first met?"

Lucas roams the shop, an appreciative gleam in his eyes. "I'm not sure what smells better. The scotch you have put away or the holy water you've got for sale." Pausing at a rack, he lifts a vial of clear liquid. "What proof is this, you think?" Popping the top off, he sniffs it. "Fifty percent, at best."

Curiosity gets the better of me. "Holy water?"

Lucas replaces the vial. "Angels can't get drunk on alcohol, but holy water," he laughs, "let's just say it's intoxicating."

I try so hard not to smile and fail.

Pointing at me, he winks. "There you go. I knew you had it in you. You're going to need it." He glances at Eloise. "You've got a witch, a shifter, and a fae coming in three, two . . ."

The bell above the door dings.

Saundra Beaumont is the first to storm in, looking like the avenging angel Lucas is supposed to be. Close on her heels is Elsmed Fairchild, a one-hundred-and-two-year-old male fae with frosty blue eyes and a bone to pick. Bringing up the rear is Ric Kasun, Havenwood Falls' sheriff and a wolf-shifter. At six foot four and built as solidly as the black Chevy truck he drives around town, he looks in no mood to play games. All of them are from old families, all of them are representatives of the Court of the Sun and the Moon, and all of them are pissed.

"Close up shop," Saundra commands Eloise. "Now."

My aunt wastes no time obeying, knocking over more of the candles in her haste to flip the open sign to closed.

Saundra turns to Lucas. "You want to explain to me why you're not standing in court right now? Why you had the audacity to summon us *here?*"

Completely unfazed, the angel circles behind the store's checkout counter, stoops to retrieve something off of the shelves built beneath, and rises with a bottle of scotch and a glass. He pours the liquid.

"Want some?" he asks. The question is met with hard stares. Lucas shrugs, downs the amber-colored liquid, and then tips the empty glass at me. "I figured the familiar setting would make this a lot easier on the girl."

Elsmed's glacial eyes swing my way. He has silver hair, a flat nose, and a long chin, and I find myself thinking he'd be just as intimidating as an iceberg as he is as a fae. "Speaking of court—"

"She didn't get the summons," Lucas interrupts. "I intercepted it."

While they argue, I stumble, catching myself. The stomach pain I'd felt when I arrived at my aunt's shop worsens. My head pounds, my skin itching. The fading bruises around my neck tingle.

Something is wrong with me.

Ric Kasun frowns, his muscles tense when he advances on the fallen angel. Even out of uniform—his broad frame in flannel, jeans, and boots—he looks every bit the sheriff this town needs. He removes a pair of sunglasses perched on his nose, revealing silvery blue eyes framed by black hair and a scruffy jaw. "There are rules in place here, Mr. Fox."

Lucas's gaze hardens, his smirk wiped away. For the first time since I've met him, he scares me. "I'm not breaking the law, Sheriff. I just changed the Court's venue. Should I remind all of you that I'm here to help your town, not hurt it?"

"We have a certain way we do things," Saundra inserts.

"I'm becoming well aware of that," Lucas mumbles. Setting down his glass, he straightens to full height, putting him eye to eye with Sheriff Kasun. "My first priority is the girl and the archdemon using her as a conduit. You don't want a demon like him anywhere near your Court." He comes around the counter, leaving nothing between him and the Court members. "Let me give you a rundown on how archdemons play games. Leviathan—Levi to make things simple and because I seriously don't like the bastard—won't set off your wards. He's not like the demons you have in residence here. He has an eternity of tricks up his sleeve. You won't know he's coming until he shows up."

My heart begins to race, and I tug at my shirt as heat washes over me. I am hot, *so very hot*, and I *never* get hot.

Ric's eyes narrow. "Talk to us, angel. Why won't our wards detect him?"

"Because he has other ways of getting into your town." Lucas's gaze finds me. "It starts with nightmares, terrible visions full of death. Then the marks come."

I can't breathe. My world has narrowed to the heat in my skin and the look Lucas gives me. Blue eyes. There are too many blue eyes in this room.

My vision blurs.

Lucas approaches me, a hazy figure in a shop full of mystical things.

"What are you doing?" I gasp, my words sounding so very far away, as if I'm yelling inside an echoing tunnel.

I want to back away, but I can't.

"Angel," Ric warns, a low growl escaping him. His wolf is on high alert.

When he reaches me, Lucas grabs the hem of my sweatshirt, fisting the material in his hands before jerking it up past my bra, his gaze locking with mine. "Don't look down."

The Court members gasp.

"Oh, my God!" Eloise exclaims. "What's happening to her?" She starts to rush toward me, but Lucas pushes me toward the counter.

"Keep your distance," he says. "You're psychic, and she's a conduit. You touch her now, and you're just as likely to suffer." He leans forward. "Deep breaths, Harper."

I inhale, exhale, and inhale again. Oxygen rushes into my system, clearing my vision and making me horrendously lightheaded.

Putting a little distance between us, his hands still wrapped in my shirt, Lucas finally gives me space enough to look down.

"Prepare for the worst," he advises.

My gaze falls, my breath catching in my throat. Shock and horror turn me mute, trapping any noises or words I'm tempted to make or say. Claw marks run across my stomach, ending just beneath my ribs.

Saundra Beaumont bears down on us, her face stormy. "What does this mean?"

"It's exactly what it looks like," Lucas replies. "Demonic possession. Well, a form of it. He's not directly inhabiting her body, but he's siphoning power and energy. When the time comes, Levi will use Harper to get into Havenwood Falls. She's his portal. By the time the wards detect him, he will have caused a lot of destruction."

My aunt begins to cry, her tears an eerie song in a tense room of silence.

"But the archdemon wants *you*, right?" Saundra asks finally, her deep brown eyes locked on Lucas.

"All because I wanted to write my name," I whisper, mostly to myself.

Lucas lets my shirt drop, but he doesn't release me, his gaze swinging to the witch. "He holds a grudge against me."

Saundra's jaw tenses. "Can you defeat him?"

"Them," Lucas corrects. "There are two demons attracted to Harper. One can trip your wards, but don't underestimate her. Because I'm not sure why I feel her, and I don't know why she's linked with the psychic."

"Two!" Eloise's sobs grow. It sounds like her heart is breaking. Maybe it is.

"Shit!" Ric swears. "This is a security nightmare!" He glances at me, and I know what he's really thinking by the sympathetic look in his eyes. *I'm* the security nightmare. His heart is too big to admit it, too big to blame me out loud.

Ric turns to Saundra. "We need to keep them out of the town. I don't have any desire to tie up with an archdemon or a stranger, but I'll be damned if I let them hurt anyone in Havenwood Falls."

"What can you do to help?" Elsmed steps forward, his disconcerting eyes studying the fallen angel. "On Saundra's request, we summoned you to fix this problem."

Lucas's gaze finds mine again. "I have some favors I plan to call in."

The way he says it—the way he *looks* at me—is oddly reassuring. His hands are warm against the skin of my waist, and I find myself struggling with the need to push him away and the desire to pull him closer. Stranger or no, he looks like salvation.

With a small wink, he releases me, and turns to Saundra. "You and your witches may have to spell a few people, but I'll do my best to keep it contained."

"And you don't know when he'll come?" Saundra asks.

"It depends on how much strength he's gained. Any advantage I have will depend on how weak being in the Infernum has made him." The look he gives her tells a thousand stories. "You know what the Infernum does, witch. You hold a key that opens a portal into part of it. It's a potent feeling finding a weakness that can trap something powerful, isn't it? I have friends in very high places. Low ones, too. I am impressed by what you've done with the Blue Dragon Dagger."

Saundra's eyes fill with understanding and wisdom too deep to fathom. I've known the Court members since I was a child, but I don't think I truly realized how much they knew about this strange world we live in. Until now. They know things I can't even fathom. Things I'm not sure it's safe for me to know. Things I wonder if I *should* know.

Saundra sighs, swipes her hands down her black business suit, and says, "Just get that devil and anyone working with him out of my town, angel."

Lucas bows, and although it comes off as sarcastic, respect flickers in his gaze. "My pleasure, my lady."

"And follow close on his heels while you're at it," Saundra adds.

Lucas grins. "Aw, I see just how much you're going to miss me."

Saundra studies him, her lips twitching. "I don't know whether you're one of the good guys or one of the bad, Lucas Fox, and that unnerves me."

"We're all walking a blurred line, witch. It often takes being bad to save the good."

Something about his words stirs the Court members. They fidget, and I wonder just how many secrets the Court of the Sun and the Moon holds.

I'm not sure I have time to care. If the nightmares I've been having the last few days and the claw marks on my flesh are any indication, I'm a ticking time bomb.

CHAPTER 6

Once the door closes behind the court members, Aunt Eloise spins, the alarm on her face turning into grim concern. "Maybe you should consider moving back in."

"No way!" The words pop out much more vehemently than I intend them to. "No." Softening my voice, I approach her, head shaking. "I can't."

"Not for good, Harper." She tugs on her earrings, and I know if she doesn't stop, she's going to make herself bleed. "Just until all of this is over."

With a touch of annoyance, she glances at a spot over my shoulder. At the counter, Lucas pours another glass of scotch.

"Don't mind me." He salutes us with the liquor.

I ignore him. "If I come back now, I'm letting them win."

The monsters are *not* allowed to win. They've taken too much from me. Innocence. Youth. Magic.

They won't take my life.

Eloise's face reddens, and a tear trickles down her cheek. She swipes at it angrily. "I promised your parents I'd do my best by you."

She starts to grab me by the arms, and then stops, her hands dropping to her sides. It's disconcerting to see her so upset. Aunt Eloise never cries; she sings Van Morrison and makes herbal remedies until everything in her world is right again.

"I don't know how to help," my aunt admits.

There's nothing worse than feeling helpless. Nothing worse than not being able to rescue the people you love the most. Nothing worse than being afraid you're going to hurt not only innocent bystanders, but the people you care about. It's a nightmare I will never wake up from.

"It's better for her in the mountains," Lucas interjects. "Less casualties if something goes wrong."

Eloise stares at him, her gaze intent. Minutes tick by like years. "Don't fail, angel," she says finally, voice wavering. "Please don't fail."

"Levi was bound to find a way to get to me eventually. If not through your niece, then another way. I promise you, I fully intend to give him the fight he deserves." He looks to me. "We should go."

"Together?" A million thoughts flood my head, and none of them are good.

Me. Him. Strangers.

Maybe he senses my unease because he comes to me, a sardonic tilt to his lips. "I like my coffee black, music that beats so hard you can feel it in your pulse, and gambling. But only if I know I'm going to win. I don't do long walks on the beach, but watching sunsets from the clouds," he shrugs, "it does it for me." He offers me his hand. "Now that you know something about me, does that help?" Frustration colors his gaze, and I don't know if I'm the reason behind it or if it's the demon haunting me.

After a moment's hesitation, my hand touches his.

He pulls me into him, startling me. Bright light flashes, and I shut my eyes against the glare.

When I open them again, we're inside my cabin in the mountains, his embrace cloaking me. He's massive, his muscular frame making me feel much, much smaller than I actually am. His heart beats against my cheek, his chest rising and falling with each breath. It's too intimate, and I have to fight the need to struggle.

"You're not used to being held, are you?" Lucas asks, head bent, his breath whispering against my neck.

Shudders race through me. "It hurts." Emotions, old and new, play a complicated game of hide and seek within me. To hide it, I push against him. "My stomach," I lie, even though it *does* pain me.

Immediately, he lets go. "Let me see it."

"What? No." I back away from him. "It's fine."

A smile flits across his face, the expression gone as fast as it appears. "Sit."

"Seriously, I'm good."

"No creams or medicines will fix demonic wounds." He urges me toward the sofa. "I can help."

When he drops to his knees in front of me, I start to shoot up, but he grips my waist, holding me in place. His hand slips under the hem of my shirt.

I look anywhere and everywhere except at him.

Cool air rushes against my skin, aggravating the raw wound and making me increasingly aware that I am not alone. His fingers run gently over my ribs.

I tense, electric tingles shooting all the way down to my toes. Birds flap frantic wings inside my stomach.

"Relax," Lucas soothes.

He touches the claw marks, and I hiss. Beneath his fingers, cool heat flares, and the pain from the injury subsides. The pad of his thumb dips toward my navel.

Hugging my middle, I fly off the sofa.

From his place on the floor, Lucas watches me. "I make you uncomfortable." It's a statement, not a question.

"I don't know. I—"

"Do you want to have sex?"

The question is so abrupt, so unexpected, that I'm pretty sure I squeak. "What?" My eyes widen. "Did you . . ." Pausing, I stare, inhale, and then, "Did you just proposition me?"

I mean, did he?

He stands, completely comfortable with himself and the situation. "I asked if you wanted to have sex."

A crazed laugh escapes me. "I don't even know you."

He shrugs, unconcerned. "I don't always know the women I sleep with."

My mouth falls open. "Are you serious right now?"

"The pleasures of the flesh are an enjoyable way for you to get over this fear you have of being touched."

The hell?

"I don't have a fear . . ." I wag a finger at him. "You know what? I don't like you."

"You'd like me much better if you had sex with me."

The snort that slips out of me is completely unrefined. "You know, that's not even worth a response."

Turning away, I busy myself by trying to start a fire. Lucas joins me, nods at the hearth, and then steps back when the wood within bursts into flames.

I glare, annoyed. "I could have done that."

"All you have to do is say no," Lucas says, and I know he's not talking about the fire.

My chin rises. "No."

He leans against the stone fireplace. "You're going to have to find a way to feel comfortable around me fast, Harper. The things that will happen to you won't be pretty. You need to be okay with me helping you with that."

"By having sex?"

"By opening yourself up in any way you feel comfortable doing so. Sex is just a fun suggestion."

Emotions swell like a tsunami inside of me, the strength of it threatening to knock me into the fire. "Do you have a lot of experience with things like this?"

"Demons or sex?"

I throw him a look.

He grins, and then sobers. "I've done a lap or two around the demonic block. Dealing with demons is complicated. Sometimes the experiences are bad. Other times, they're surprisingly good. I even call a few demons friends."

This, I find interesting. "The good demons? There's a few in town. There's one, she—"

"There are *decent* ones. Never confuse decent with good." Memories spark in his gaze, the resulting smile crinkling the corners of his eyes. "Or maybe it's just the ones I've come into contact with. The demons I know wouldn't appreciate being called good. I doubt they'd even appreciate being called decent."

The demon talk is becoming too much for me.

"They call me a generational curse," I blurt out, stepping back. Lucas keeps his distance, the flames from the hearth shadowing his face. "My father is psychic, but my mother was mortal."

Shut up, Harper, I tell myself.

My heart couldn't give a shit about what my logic thinks. I never get a chance to babble, except with Eloise. Having Lucas here is like having a therapist I don't have to pay for, who's being forced to stay and listen. Bless him. "My parents had trouble getting pregnant, so it was this huge thing when they discovered they were having me."

Pausing, I go into the kitchen and pull out a loaf of bread from a box on the counter. It's homemade sourdough wrapped just for me by the supe who works in the bakery section of our local supermarket. No labels. "Do you eat grilled cheese?"

He told me to be comfortable. Grilled cheese makes me comfortable.

Lucas's brows arch. "What happened to your parents?"

Sighing, I rest my hands on the counter. "Something went wrong with the pregnancy. I wasn't going to make it. The doctors told her it would be best to terminate. For her sake." My heart breaks for a woman I never knew. "My mother had a breakdown over it. She couldn't accept the idea of losing me, so Dad took it before the Court and begged them to do something—a spell, a ritual, or anything—to save me. They refused."

I swallow hard. "You know, I hated the Court for that when I found out. By then, I was ten years old. My aunt sat me down and said," changing my voice, I try to imitate Eloise, "'You've got to understand, Harper. It's not a simple thing trying to cheat death. It often hurts others worse than the person dying.'"

Abandoning the bread, I move back into the living room. "My aunt is right. She has this uncanny knack for being right about things." I cringe. "My parents heard of a sorceress in Louisiana who did black magic. So they went to her. She saved my mother's pregnancy, but what she neglected to tell them was that, by doing so, my mother would be forfeiting her life and I'd be hounded by evil."

Lucas remains unmoving by the fire. He's too still, as if he's a sculpture rather than an angel. "And your father?"

"When my mother died in childbirth, he blamed himself for her death. It was too much on him, so he left. My aunt raised me." My chin dips, my gaze tracing the wood grain on the floor. "I tried to find my dad a few years ago. He's in California. Married with two kids. He doesn't remember Havenwood Falls, my mother, or me. The Court protects the town by ensuring people who leave here forget it." My gaze finds Lucas. "It's for the best. I think he's happy now."

"He knows something is missing. A spell can't take that away," Lucas says.

Swallowing past a sudden thickness in my throat, I ask, "How do you know?"

"Because I have a lot of practice with magic and a deep history with witches."

He steps away from the fire. The afternoon light from the one window in the living room grazes his face.

I haven't bothered with turning on the lights, and I don't know if it's because I'm more comfortable in the natural light from outside or because I've grown used to dark corners.

Firelight and slanted sunshine transform the room into something wholly unrealistic and yet entirely too real.

Lucas stops before me. "Magic and the supernatural tend to make mortals uncomfortable. Even dangerous. No one likes feeling weak." He glances at the window and at the snow-touched mountains beyond. White brilliance. "Those with differences have to protect themselves. They have to do things in order to protect their families, things that don't sit well with them, but magic has its limitations. It can get rid of memories, but the emptiness the memories leave behind is always there, lurking."

"You sound like you should get along better with Saundra Beaumont—with *all* of the Court—better than you seemed to today."

Lucas's gaze swings back to me. "Let's just say we understand each other, but I'm less willing to confine myself to one place."

He leans forward, putting him so close I can make out every detail of his face. It's unnaturally perfect, rugged and covered in stubble. Just enough to be sexy.

He's a mirage. I don't know how I know it, I just do. Maybe it's the psychic in me, the psychic I could have been if I hadn't been cursed. Looking at Lucas is like staring at a man who never changes. A man who never has to sleep or eat. A man who never has to shave. A man who just *is.*

"What kind of angel were you?" I whisper.

"What kind am I?" he corrects. "Being fallen doesn't make me any less of what I was." His gaze searches mine, and then, "A Seraph. I am a

Seraph. The best and worst kind of angel." There's nothing human in the way he looks when he says it.

"What made you fall?"

We are nearly nose to nose when he replies, "I murdered a man."

If hearts could stop beating, mine would quit. Instead, it races, as if beating faster can get it far away from the creature in front of me. Except my body traps my heart, forcing it to face a moment it wants to avoid.

Hearts are cowardly things.

Bodies are shockingly resilient.

I don't run. I don't run because I've murdered a man, too, and although I wasn't wholly responsible—hell, I'd only been a child—the guilt remains. I *feel* like I murdered him.

"I can't judge someone for something I've done," I breathe, surprising him.

He straightens, amusement lightening his eyes. "Bonding over murder. I'd say that's a first."

He doesn't ask me who I killed. Either the Court has supplied him with the information or he doesn't care.

I don't care for the humor. "Did you mean to do it?" We may have something in common, but I never meant to hurt anyone.

For a moment, I think he's not going to answer, but then he touches my face, startling me. "I was trying to save someone not too unlike you. He was hurting her. I shouldn't have interfered. I wasn't supposed to interfere, but I did. He's dead, and I'm fallen."

From the way he drops his gaze, I know he hadn't intended to answer me. Maybe he'd planned to lie.

"Thank you." If I'm stuck with an angel who's supposed to help me fight demons, I can at least appreciate his honesty.

"What's it going to be like when the archdemon comes?" I ask out of nowhere. "If I'm a portal for him, will he," I look down at my stomach, "burst out of me?"

If I'm going to be a conduit for a demon, then I want to go into it as knowledgeable about it as possible. Knowledge is power.

Lucas laughs, the sound deep and thrilling. "You must read a lot of science fiction."

"*Listen*," I correct. "I listen to a lot of science fiction. On audiobook." My hands press against my stomach, and I know by the way it doesn't pain me that the claw marks are gone. "Will it hurt?"

I try to hide the fear I'm feeling, but my voice cracks.

Lucas places his hand over mine on my stomach, squeezing my fingers just enough to be reassuring. "He won't physically burst out of you, but he will torment you. Be prepared for that. He'll use your energy to bring himself into the physical world, so he'll need you near."

Relief is a pleasant feeling that's all too fleeting.

I won't be giving birth to any grotesque beings, but the demon *can* harm me. As a psychic from a long line of psychics, I know enough about spirits to know they have the ability to harm someone they're attached to. The physical stuff is rarer—it takes a lot of energy for a spirit to manifest—but it's possible.

I have another question, but I leave it unasked.

If this demon is strong enough to nearly strangle me in Jeanine Turner's office and claw me at my aunt's shop, what's to stop him from killing me?

"How about that grilled cheese sandwich now?" I ask instead.

Lucas smiles. "Okay."

CHAPTER 7

The last thing I remember before falling asleep is the way the sun moved over the living room as it set, cloaking the house in darkness, the fire in the hearth crackling.

Lucas sat on the end of my couch while I curled against the opposite end, a blanket wrapped around my shoulders. Empty plates rested on the kitchen counter, the silence in the room a lullaby urging my eyes to close.

I fought it, but in the end, weariness won out over wariness.

The angel watching me couldn't be any worse than the archdemon haunting me.

On the heels of another nightmare, debilitating nausea wakes me, and I find myself in my bed, my bare feet tangled in sheets I've apparently been fighting. My room is dark, the window to the side of my queen-sized four poster bed revealing a snowy ground under a star-dotted sky.

My breath comes fast, and I swallow the rising bile in my throat.

The nausea worsens.

Kicking myself free of the sheets, I tumble out of my bed, my knees hitting the floor hard before I drag myself toward the bathroom adjoining the bedroom.

I gag.

Hands lift me, and I struggle.

"Shh," Lucas's voice soothes. "It's me."

The bathroom light clicks on, casting a glow over soft yellow walls and ivory-tiled floors. Sunshine and sunflowers.

My stomach cramps, and I fight the angel holding me. "Please."

He sets me down in front of the toilet just as the vomiting begins. It comes so hard and so fast, I can't breathe through the heaving. Worse yet, blood gushes from my mouth. Straight blood, the metallic taste of it making the nausea sweep me in increasing waves.

My hands grip the porcelain, desperate for the coolness.

Lucas sits behind me, his long legs swallowing me, his thighs embracing me. Pulling my hair back, he fists it in one of his hands.

"I'm dying," I manage to gasp.

"No," he assures me, "but you're going to feel like you are."

The cramps subside, and I sag against his chest, too afraid and spent to be embarrassed. Lucas leans away from me and reaches into a cabinet under the sink. A pile of folded washcloths sits on a shelf. Taking one, he squeezes it in his fist. When he places it against my face, it's wet. The cool moisture feels so good against my heated flesh; I don't even care how he dampened the material.

"Have you been going through my house?" I ask weakly, accepting the cloth.

He drops his arm and slides it around my waist. "Preparation."

Silence.

The embarrassment finally washes over me, thick and uncomfortable. "Oh, God."

Lucas's arm tightens. "It's only going to get worse. The stronger he becomes—the more energy he pulls—the weaker and sicker you're going to be. I can't stop him until he's here. I can't go where he is."

A solitary tear slips down my cheek. It's all I care to give the being tormenting me. One tear packed full of fear and resentment.

"I bet this makes me the first girl you've ever watched vomit blood," I say, trying to lighten the mood. It comes off too soft to be funny.

Lucas combs my hair with his fingers. "You're the first girl who's ever channeled a demon with a vendetta against me. You shouldn't have been drawn into this. If I was able to enter where he is, you wouldn't be his way of getting to me. You also wouldn't be my way of reaching him."

Something in his voice catches me off guard. "Do I hear regret?"

"Don't push it," he mumbles.

I can't help it; I laugh.

Nausea slams into me again, out of nowhere, and the laughter ends on choking sobs.

Lucas rushes to help. I heave over and over until there's nothing left. Until I'm a crumpled mess of weakness. As limp as the washcloth.

Blood and anguish.

A burning pain replaces the nausea in my gut, and I cry out.

Growling, Lucas stands, dragging me up with him. "Damn you, Levi."

Without bothering to ask, he tugs my shirt up and off. Drained, my head hangs, my gaze falling on fresh claw marks on my skin, deeper than the ones that had been there before. Blood drips from the wound, the liquid soaking into the band of my jeans.

Lucas unbuttons my pants.

"What are you doing?" I try struggling, but spots dance before my eyes.

"Remember earlier when I suggested we have sex?" he asks while dragging my jeans down over my thighs. "Maybe you ought to have taken me up on the offer. Into the shower with you." He leaves my bra and underwear on, but everything else goes.

Near the bathroom's entrance is a small stand-up shower. Lucas slides the beveled glass door open and steps inside, bringing me with him. The stall is barely big enough for one person, much less two, but this doesn't deter him.

"Hold on for me, Harper." Resting my hand on the bar inside, he releases me, and with a swiftness that doesn't help my lightheadedness, he sheds his clothes, chucks them outside, and slides the door shut.

"What—?" He turns on the shower, and the initial blast of cold water tears a yelp out of me that drowns out any protests.

Pulling me against him, *all* of him, Lucas slides his hands over my wound. "I can't stop the nausea, but *this* I can fix."

Cool heat flares where he touches me. Blood mingles with water at our feet.

The world spins away from me, making all of this seem surreal: his hands against my skin, the warming water pounding us, the blood, and the sensations pouring through me.

Lucas slips his fingers into the sides of my panties, and when I don't fight him, he slides them down before unsnapping my bra.

His arms circle me, steam rising around us.

I'm ashamed to admit my brain is too foggy and my body too weak to remember much about the shower. He washes me, gently stroking my skin while silently cursing the demon under his breath. He also makes promises to me. Promises to avenge everything Levi has done.

Afterward, he enfolds me in a terry cloth towel, helps me brush my teeth, and carries me to the bed. I'm a limp doll with a sodden heart.

The mattress dips when he sets me on it, and I clutch his bare arms. "Stay . . . please."

His blue eyes darken.

Unlike me, he's not wearing a towel. He's comfortable in his nudity, comfortable with *himself* in a way most people can only hope to be, and I draw strength from that.

He climbs into the bed in front of me, and I curl into his chest. His arm slides over my waist, my towel the only thing separating us.

He's warm, and even though he couldn't stop my vomiting, he feels safe.

Sudden tears leak down my cheeks, the ferocity of them frightening. Shaking me. These tears have nothing to do with the demon and everything to do with me. These tears are deeper. Personal.

For the first time since I was a child, I let someone hold me. And he's not only someone, he's a stranger. A *Stranger.*

Ever since my father left Havenwood Falls and I accidentally caused the death of the man in town, I have pushed people away. Even Aunt Eloise. For years, I stepped out of her hugs because anything longer than a brief touch was too much.

"Let someone help you," she had begged.

I was scared of hurting people and of getting hurt.

Sobs wrack my body. I cry for Eloise. I cry for my mother. I cry for my father. I cry for *myself.* Years of tears.

Tipping my face up gently, Lucas studies my tear-stained eyes, and then kisses me, his lips closing over mine, his warm mouth catching my teardrops.

Tender. Soothing. Fleeting.

Gone as quick as it began.

"Quit thinking," he whispers. "Pain can be so deep that it's hard to bring the people you're too close to into that hurt. Sometimes it takes giving it to a stranger before you can open up to someone else."

"How—"

"Just trust I know."

I stare at him through eyes swollen from tears and madness. "Do you have anyone you're close to?"

"A few."

"Someone you love?"

"Friends."

I let the word sink in, and then, "Have you ever been in love?"

"No." The answer comes too fast.

"You're a high-ranking fallen angel, and you're telling me after all of the years you've existed—"

"An eternity."

I glare, but fatigue takes all of the bite out of it. "You could have kept the eternity part to yourself because now that just makes this," I point from him to me, "weird."

He chuckles. "No, it makes me experienced."

"Not helping. Now I'm self-conscious." My lips curl into a smile. "And you're changing the subject. You can't tell me that in an *eternity* you haven't fallen in love at least once."

With his finger, Lucas traces a line from my forehead to my nose. "Three times," he admits carefully. "Once before my fall. Two after. A mortal in the middle ages, a demon, and a witch."

"What happened?" I ask.

His finger drops to my lips. "The mortal died. The witch and the demon fell in love with each other."

I stare, unable to speak.

"And you, my little psychic?"

My head shakes.

"No one?"

Taking his finger, I remove it from my lips. "It's hard to do relationships when you have to limit yourself so much. No cell phones, no texting each other, no movie theaters, or restaurants with fancy-scripted menus." Reaching out, I caress his face, surprising myself with my boldness. He leans into my touch, the gesture boosting my confidence. "I had crushes. I even tried the whole boyfriend thing, but," my fingers run through the stubble on his face, fascinated with the roughness, "it didn't work out."

"What about when you were in school?"

I shrug, one bare shoulder rising. "I was kept separated. There are two high schools in Havenwood Falls: Havenwood Falls High and the Sun and Moon Academy. The latter is a private school for supernatural students who don't or can't fit into the public school system. Guess where I went?" My lips curl. "They tried teaching me to read and write. I learned, but not without consequences. It took everything the Court's witches had to keep the evil things I kept channeling contained. So, they developed a new way to teach me. I listened to audio textbooks and took verbal tests. Each of the Court members worked with me. Alone. I owe them so much."

Tears prick my eyes again. "This town . . . it's everything to so many people. To me." I inhale. "Saundra Beaumont and her granddaughter, Addie, helped teach me science by doing experiments with me. Addie's a year older than me, and it helped that I wasn't the only child. The shifters would let me join them in the woods, tracking and learning. What I couldn't learn outside the classroom, they found other creative ways to teach me. There's a coffee shop in town, Coffee Haven, owned by a fae, Willow Fairchild. She displays art from local artists in the shop, and she'd bring pieces to show me outside. All kinds. Oil. Water color. Photography. I fell in love with the photography. Then . . ." My words trailing off, I cover my eyes. "You need to tell me to shut up."

His hand cups my hip, and even through the towel, the touch burns. "Talk, Harper. Talk as much and as long and as big as you need to."

I drop my hands, my incredulous gaze finding his face. "Where did you come from?" He just doesn't seem real.

"From Hell," he answers soberly. "From Hell and Heaven and everything in between. From myth and legend. From gods and goddesses. From the beginning of time until the end."

"Why does that sound sad?" I ask.

"Because eternity is a very long time."

Now I know why this feels so good and hurts so much. We are both lonely strangers. To each other, and maybe even to ourselves.

This time, I kiss him, my hands framing his face, my lips tentative. He opens for me, and our tongues slide together, the sensation sending a pool of heat to my core.

His hand tightens on my hip, his fingers digging into the towel.

My fingers slip into his hair, and suddenly I don't care if I don't know him. I don't care if he isn't human.

He runs his hand up my side, his fingers brushing the edge of my breast, and I arch against him.

"Harper," he whispers.

"Please," I whisper back.

He undoes the towel I'm wearing and replaces it with his skin. His mouth leaves mine, his lips leaving a trail of fire down my jaw, my neck, and my breasts.

I close my eyes because the feel of him is so much better than anything I could have imagined. He doesn't demand anything. He simply gives, and I wonder if it's because I'm not experienced.

What is happening with my life?

This isn't the way I saw any of my firsts.

I certainly don't hear any Van Morrison music.

Instead, I *feel* everything. The hard length of him against my thigh. His hands sliding over parts of me I've never shared with anyone else. His mouth creating heat in places that make my face burn.

Waves of pleasure so intense it's almost painful.

When his mouth returns to mine and he presses into me, I meet his thrust with my hips, my body tense because I expect pain.

There isn't any.

Startled, I meet his gaze.

Holding himself above me, his arms caging me in, he says, "Relax. This much I can do, too. You've endured enough pain."

The tension leaves my body, and he thrusts deeper, my body taking all of him.

My legs wrap around his waist, my fingers digging into his shoulders.

"Oh, God," I breathe.

Chuckling, he kisses the side of my neck, and then whispers, "Now let me show you what heaven feels like."

CHAPTER 8

*L*ucas isn't in the bed when I wake.

I rise with the sun, my body sore, my mind so full of thoughts I don't quite know where to put them all, and I'm glad he's gone.

Too much, too fast, I think.

First house. First time having sex. First time having sex with an *angel*. First one-night stand. Vomiting blood. All within days, even hours and minutes, of each other, because I'm an over-achiever like that.

I grab the pillow next to me, stuff my face into it, and scream. A good scream, not the bad kind. Unlike Aunt Eloise, I have no desire to take back my virginity.

If anything, I want to thank Lucas. It might not have been what I imagined—sex with someone I've had at least three dates with or a guy I am head over heels in love with—but it was everything I needed. Right now. At this moment.

Throwing my legs over the side of the bed, I rush to my closet, quickly donning the usual skinny jeans and sweatshirt. Heavy coat. A knit cap. Solid colors. No words.

My camera bag sits on the living room floor, and I sling it onto my shoulder.

Everything outside looks and feels new. The snow on the ground, the white powder dusting the trees, the way the rising sun paints the sky a rainbow of blues, pinks, and purples. The way the air smells, crisp and tinged with smoke.

Taking my camera out of my bag, I turn back to my cabin, focus the shot, and shoot a picture of the arched front door.

"I've heard of people skipping out on one night stands, but never on me. I think I'm offended."

Smiling, I spin to find Lucas standing in the snow, his hands cradling two cups of coffee, and I know by the way he's gripping one of them, he's hiding a logo.

"You went into town?" I ask.

"More like blinked in and out. Here." He hands me a plain white Styrofoam cup.

The awkwardness of our situation slams into me like a high-speed train. "I don't drink—"

"It's hot chocolate."

Accepting the cup with my free hand, I sniff the contents. "How did you know? I didn't tell you . . ." My gaze swings to Lucas, then back to the cup, my eyebrows practically shooting to my hairline. "How *did* you know?"

His silence is telling.

I groan. "Oh, no . . . don't tell me."

He smirks. "It's an angel thing. Well, a Seraph thing, though a few other castes can do it as well. If it makes you feel better, I can't really read your thoughts. I don't know why. Maybe the demons? You've trained yourself to block out demons for so long, it's like trying to break through an incredibly sophisticated security system. I only get small things from you. Things like the fear of touch. Hot chocolate."

He walks toward me, and he's so brilliant surrounded by the snow and the sky, I rush to set my cup in the snow. From a crouch, I lift my camera.

The *click* is loud in the still morning.

"So, all those things I told you," I ask, still crouching, "you didn't see them in my head?"

He crouches in front of me. "No, and it's refreshing having to guess. Most people make it too easy." Touching my camera, he raises his brows. "You know this won't develop, right?"

"The picture of you?" I'm unable to hide my disappointment. "Why?"

"Seraph means fiery one. The only thing you're going to get on that film is a walking blaze. Since I'm fallen, you'll get a touch of blue fire in there, too."

Standing, I peer down at him. "You like being fallen, don't you?"

"What makes you think that?"

"The way your eyes light up when you say it."

He stands, instantly towering over me. "It bothered me at first, but over the years I've learned to embrace it and what it means. Blurred lines exist for a reason. Some of the best warriors exist in the gray area." Tapping his head as if it's a treasure chest full of knowledge, he smiles. "Half your town's Court among them. Besides," his gaze slides over the snow-covered mountain, "I've been fortunate enough to fight alongside beings and people I would not have fought with if I was still a Risen." His eyes find mine. "And the ones I fought alongside were in the right. Not all demons are bad. Not all angels are good. Not all people are innocent."

Fierce passion makes his eyes glow, lightening them until they are almost colorless, and I suddenly understand why he's a fiery one.

Stooping, he picks up my hot cocoa. "Come on, I've got you a present, and if you're in the mood to take pictures, it's the perfect place for it."

He saunters away.

I rush to catch up with him, camera in hand. "There isn't a place on Mt. Souza, or any mountains around Havenwood Falls for that matter, I don't know."

"Oh, it's not a part of the mountain. It's more of a thing."

We march through the snow, hitting a trail just behind the cabin. My boots leave deep prints in the white powder. His boots leave no marks whatsoever.

"Another Seraph thing?" I ask, indicating the snow. "Just what all *can* you do? Other than healing demonic wounds, vanishing, and reading thoughts."

Lucas glances at the ground. "A lot." When he lifts his head, his eyes are shuttered. "Too much." The tone of his voice tells me everything I need to know. Despite his arrogance, Lucas is not a flashy angel.

Reaching the top of an incline, he turns and offers me his hand. Even though it isn't steep, I accept his help.

A shallow hollow spreads out before us, mountain slopes rising on three sides, majestic and full of power. A cold, pine-scented wind reddens my cheeks before whistling into the valley.

Nature sings.

"One of my favorite places," I breathe, lifting my camera.

"Not yet," Lucas says, stopping me. He gazes out over the space, and then points. "There."

From the edge of the valley, something lopes toward us, a dark blur on snow. "What is that?"

"A favor." He grins. "From a friend."

I edge toward the angel, unease trickling down my spine. "Is that . . . *oh.*"

From the snow, a lion approaches us, his face surrounded by a magnificent fiery mane, his eyes narrowed. Wings protrude from his back, the appendages large enough to envelop him. The closer he draws to us, the more magnificent he becomes.

I blink, and he's in front of me.

Words fail me.

Resting on his haunches in the snow, the lion studies me. Like Lucas, he leaves no tracks in the snow. I am tiny compared to him. Strangely, he doesn't dwarf Lucas at all.

"Meet the Destroyer," Lucas introduces.

"Destroyer?" I whisper, awed. I have met too many supernatural beings in my life to be cowed, but impressed . . . oh, I am most certainly impressed.

Lucas pats the beast on the shoulder. "Or Desi for short."

The lion glares. "You go too far, angel."

"Don't be fooled," Lucas tells me, ignoring the creature. "He likes it."

"What . . . how . . ." Inhaling, I try again. "*Where* did he come from?" My gaze flies to the lion. "*You*, I mean. Where did you come from?"

Lucas answers for him, a secret smile on his lips. "A very powerful gargoyle friend of mine out of France. He has a thing for collecting ancient weapons."

"Weapon? *That* does not look like a weapon!" The lion growls, and I step back. "No offense or anything. I just . . ." I shake my head. "I think I'm going to shut up now."

"Into the mace, Desi," Lucas snaps, startling me.

Grumbling, the lion stretches out in the snow, folds his wings over himself, and then vanishes. *Poof.* Gone. In his place is an intricately carved wooden club, the end of it covered in bronze thorns.

Time out.

"Did," I gesture at the club, "*that* lion just turn into a baseball bat on steroids?"

The mountains echo when Lucas laughs.

Setting our drinks in the snow, Lucas swipes the steroid-bat off the ground and offers it to me. "It's a mace, a much more popular weapon a long time ago. It's yours, for now."

I stare at it. "Not that I don't appreciate this, but I wasn't expecting to wake up this morning to hot cocoa and a new pet, *er*, mace."

"He'll be an invaluable ally for you."

Tucking my camera into the bag on my shoulder, I let Lucas place the weapon in my hands. It's surprisingly light considering it was just a massive, flying male lion.

"I don't like the way you're giving this to me," I say quietly. "This gift comes with too many unsaid things."

Reaching out, he tucks a strand of hair behind my ear before pulling my knit cap down over it. "You are stronger than you know, Harper. You don't get ruffled easily. You take pain better than most mortals I've met. You've been locked away from your abilities out of fear, and when that fear is gone, you're going to discover a whole new woman locked inside of you, too. It takes an awful lot of power to keep a Seraph out of your head. Until then," he winks, "Desi here will be a friend. He's a sentient weapon, which means you can fight with him, use him for information, or even let him fight for you when you can't. I'd teach you how to use a sword or some other form of defense, but we're running out of time."

"What about you?" I ask, my hands gripping the weapon. "Couldn't you use the mace?"

Lucas ducks his head. "Seraphs are nearly invincible. I say nearly because we do have weaknesses. Not many, but we do. If Leviathan is threatening me, he's got something he knows will harm me." At my look of alarm, he tips my chin up. "I'll destroy him no matter what happens to me. This has been a long time coming. This has nothing to do with your town or you. It's not your fault."

I'm not worried about the demon's destruction; I'm worried about

Lucas. He may have charged into my life too quickly, like a flame sparking, but now that he's here, I want to know more about him. I want to know more about what and who he is. I want *time*. My abilities have always left me with little time. Scrawl a message to a guy in town. He dies. Scrawl a message threatening an angel, and my life becomes a fast-paced action novel. In audio.

I hug the weapon to myself. "What did you do to the archdemon?"

Lucas glances at the valley beyond. "When the world was ancient, Leviathan was considered a god. He was worshipped as one. His need for power, his greed, and his cruelty grew. His possessed followers were sacrificing humans for him, specifically young virgins. In his bid for supremacy, he nearly wiped out whole cities of mortals. Archdemons are a pain in the ass. For even their own kind." His gaze returns to mine. "This was the time of the gods, of the Greeks, of the Romans, and of great power. Before I fell, I was commanded to take down Leviathan before he caused more destruction. The battle wasn't an easy one. It took me and a legion of warriors to take down Levi and his minions." His eyes go distant. "A dragon of the heavens against a dragon of the seas and the land. In the end, I managed to lock him away in the Infernum, a dark place for very powerful and dangerous supernaturals who are hard to kill."

I stare, awed. "You felled a god."

"I felled an archdemon who wanted to be a god, and now he wants retribution."

If the morning was cold before, it's frigid now.

I should say things like, "No, you can't fight him!" Or at least beg him to leave Havenwood Falls, but I don't.

In retrospect, sex kind of foiled things because now I feel something for him and that complicates everything.

I also keep my mouth shut because he's right. This is his battle with an old enemy, and I am simply the tool to make it happen.

"What can I do to help?" I ask. "You know, other than bleed everywhere?"

Respect fills his gaze. "Find a way past your fears. There is unimaginable power in you. I sense it."

The mace in my hand shudders, and I nearly drop it, a shriek escaping me.

"Desi senses it, too," Lucas adds, chuckling. "Now for a suggestion.

Your bed was much, much warmer than this mountain. If you catch my meaning."

I throw him a look. "Do you even feel the cold?"

"No, but admit it." He leans close. "Bed has a nice poetic feel to it. Besides, it's Thanksgiving."

His words paralyze me. "What did you say?" Oh, God! My aunt! With everything going on, the date completely slipped my mind. "We need to go!" I wave the mace. "Make us do the whole blink in and blink out thing."

Lucas watches, amused. "I don't really do the holidays."

"Why?" I ask, aghast. "What's not to like? Food, fam—"

Family. My thoughts cut me off. Do Seraphs even have families?

"Harper," Lucas warns, grabbing for me.

I feel the gush before I see the blood pouring out of my face.

Ripping off his button-up shirt, Lucas stuffs it beneath my nose. I clutch at the material, and the mace falls to the blood-speckled snow at our feet.

"I'm sorry," I say to Desi, my voice nasal because of the shirt.

Resting a large hand on the back of my head, Lucas presses me against him. "Don't worry about the mace. He's been ordered to stay with you. Trust me, he finds his own way."

Blood soaks the shirt, and I sag against Lucas. "How has this not killed me?"

"You're weak because Levi is drawing on your energy. You're not dead because it's not your blood."

It takes a moment for his words to sink in, but when they do, I recoil, pure horror crashing down on me. "What?" I panic into the shirt, because who wouldn't? "What do you mean it's not my blood?"

"You stay calm when you think it's your blood, but you get all up in arms when it's someone else's?"

I push away from him, still clutching the shirt. "Lucas! That's like pissing out someone else's urine!"

He reaches for me. "Let's get you cleaned up."

"Whose blood is it?" I insist.

Lucas inhales, his gaze settling on mine. "The condemned. It's the blood of the condemned in the Infernum. Levi can't sacrifice humans, so he's sacrificing the condemned imprisoned with him so he can build enough strength through their deaths and your energy to escape. I don't know how he's doing it, but I know it's not your blood."

My knees go weak, but I hold my ground. "There's no way to stop him from doing this?"

"Not without going into the Infernum, and there are some places even Seraphs can't go. Escaping it is one thing; entering it is another."

"Has anyone ever escaped it before?" I don't think I want to know this answer.

"No."

My vision blurs, and I stumble away from him to lean against a tree. My hands are covered in blood, and it's not my own.

Lucas appears next to me. "The condemned suffer more than you could ever know. Death is relief. Even if it's brief. They won't stay dead. Remember what I told you about the Infernum, Harper. It's a prison for supernaturals who are nearly impossible to kill. Like archdemons." He pauses, letting that sink in before adding, "For creatures like me."

My gaze flashes to his face, Levi's words potent when I recall them. *You will have a place in Hell, Lucas Fox. Cast and chained in the Infernum of darkness. Death to the messenger. Death to those who give her sanctuary.*

"That's what he plans to do to you," I whisper.

Silence, and then, "Let's get you cleaned up."

A new resolve fills me. "Today, you're doing the holidays." He pulls back, surprised. "I may bleed everywhere, and it may be the most uncomfortable meal I have ever had, but you are damn well doing the holidays today, Lucas."

If I'm going to bleed other creatures' blood, and Lucas is prepping for a fight that may cost him more than he gains, then I'm damn sure going to show him what it means to be human.

CHAPTER 9

*A*fter returning to my cabin to clean up, Lucas blinks us to my aunt's basement apartment.

Below her shop, the apartment is an open and airy area with lots of recessed lighting to make up for the lack of windows. Stained concrete floors span the entire space, all of the rooms open to each other except for the two bedrooms. A vibrant multi-colored kitchen connects to a simple dining room with a farm table covered in artwork. The dining room joins a living room with wildly painted walls and a sofa and a recliner, each of the furniture pieces sporting gauzy scarves and strange-looking dolls. Two doors to the back of the space lead into the bedrooms. Candles are displayed on every available surface.

Eloise is in the middle of pulling a small turkey out of her oven when we appear, and she shrieks, dropping it.

Lucas catches the pan bare-handed in mid-air, places it on the kitchen's small counter, and smiles. Evidently, he's also immune to heat.

"You couldn't use the door?" Eloise asks, holding her chest.

"The angel doesn't have any manners," I tease.

Still shaken, Eloise glances from me to Lucas and then me again. "I wasn't sure you would come, but—"

I rush to embrace her, cutting off her words.

She stiffens in my arms, unused to me hugging or seeking comfort from her. Her scent of gingerbread and honey invades my senses. She smells like home. It doesn't matter that I was here only yesterday. Today, even though I am unsure about everything, I feel more confident than I have in years.

Relaxing, Eloise hugs me back, her hand stroking my hair. "Harper," she whispers in my ear.

Today, I am thankful for her.

Lucas pulls me away, regret coloring his eyes. "It's not safe," he reminds me. "I don't know how closely tied your psychic abilities are to hers."

Eloise clears her throat, turning away so she can swipe at her eyes, and guilt swamps me. I wasted too many years letting my fears and grief distance us. I doubt I'll ever feel natural around people, but my aunt is different.

Her, I should have tried harder with.

If all of this ends well, I *will* try harder.

Eloise faces us, all smiles again, although she casts a lot of ill-at-ease glances at Lucas. "I'm glad you came. I cooked enough for three meals. On purpose. Because who really wants to cook more than twice a year?"

She's lying. She loves to cook.

"Can I help?" I ask.

She ushers us into the dining room. "No! You sit." Her gaze slides to Lucas. "Both of you."

For years, every time Aunt Eloise would get stressed out about something, she would grab a box of paints and brushes, sit at the table, and create art until she was spent. The table is now a collage of anxiety-ridden graffiti. Pictures as simple as stars and as difficult as human faces fan out across the wooden surface. When she ran out of room on the table, she started on the walls.

The pictures *are* my aunt. They are her emotions, her thoughts, and her fears. My face is among the chaos, and I think it's a perfect place for it to be.

"How are things going?" Eloise asks.

Rushing back and forth, she fills plates before setting them down before us. My aunt may prefer making herbal concoctions, but she is an amazing cook. She says it's a way to express herself. Like the painted table.

"Stop," I demand. "Sit. If we need anything else, we'll get it."

She sits.

In a long, tiered peasant skirt, a strawberry-red top, and her auburn hair pulled up in a messy bun, Eloise looks young. Or *would,* if not for the circles under her eyes and the tight lines around her mouth.

"I made it through the night okay," I assure her.

She sinks her fork into her food and then stops. "Why my niece?" she asks, her gaze finding Lucas.

Because I wrote my name, I think.

Eloise stares at him hard, as if she's challenging him to a visual game of thumb war. It's not about who blinks first; it's about whose stare is stronger. "Angel?"

He leans back in his chair. He's too big for the farm table. It's like looking at an adult trying to sit at a kid's table, and yet he makes it look *not* ridiculous.

"Which question do you want me to answer first? The one about Levi or the one about her virginity?" Lucas asks.

"What?" I glance between them, horrified. Guilt takes up residence in Eloise's eyes. "You did a reading on me?" Realizing she hadn't asked the questions aloud, I throw in, "You know he can read thoughts?"

"Last night, I went to see Saundra," she replies, still staring at the angel. "It was educational to say the least. Afterward, I asked for a little guidance from the spirits."

Lucas raises his brows, impressed. "I'm developing a new respect for psychics and your tenacity."

"My niece?" Eloise persists.

"Levi is a tyrant. I don't get confused often, and when I do, it pisses me off. I don't know how he's doing what he is. I've seen a lot of demonic possessions over the years. This isn't a possession." He shakes his head. "It's like he's using her as a sacrificial altar, bleeding victims on her skin. That shouldn't be possible. He's slashing his victims. Each time he does it, it slashes her. Then he bleeds them."

My gaze falls to the table and to the food growing cold. Without looking at either of them, I eat. Stress wins out over the steal-my-appetite gruesome details. I already know I'm not bleeding my own blood. The other information is new to me, but I sense they're theories he must be throwing back and forth in his head.

"As for her virginity," he pauses, and I know he's looking at me. I refuse to look up. "She's a beautiful woman. Consenting adults. And—"

"You were protecting me," I finish for him. I should have known, and honestly, I did suspect it after he told me the story of Levi and his penchant for sacrificing virgins.

"Harper—" my aunt begins.

"I'm not surprised." I'm not. It doesn't shock me that she knows about what happened the night before. It doesn't surprise me that Lucas had sex with me as much to protect me as he did out of need and desire. Everything comes back to me—my curse and the things everyone around me has to do to fix it or protect me.

None of it surprises me.

I've been living under a microscope my entire life. What would surprise me is living *out* from under a microscope.

"You've got to know a good song for this one," I tell Eloise. "Come on, hit me with it."

When I look up, she's staring at me. Maybe she wants me to be fazed by all of this. Maybe she expects me to be upset. Maybe I should be. Thing is, I may not be doing cartwheels over all of the bad shit happening, but I'm glad I slept with Lucas. It let me connect with someone, and doing that is teaching me to connect with others. Maybe my first wasn't movie-of-the-week material, but it was an awakening. I can't regret that.

Slowly, she smiles. "Stranded."

The lyrics play in my head, and I smile back. "Now, *that* one feels like me." I glance at Lucas. "You're supposed to eat when there's a holiday. Like, a lot." He hasn't touched his food, and I add, "Even if you don't have to."

His gaze searches my face, his expression unreadable, and I'm thrown by how *deeply* he studies me.

A thousand years pass in one stare.

The sound of my aunt's chair scraping the floor drags me back into the present. "What the hell?" she exclaims. Abruptly, she stumbles away from the table, and then points to the end of it. "What the hell is that?"

There, resting in a seat, is Desi, the weird pet that turns into a badass baseball bat. Lucas *did* say it would find its way to me.

I sigh. "Just accept that my life is really weird right now."

Eloise circles the table, giving Desi a wide berth while eyeing the bronze protrusions on the weapon. "There's weird, and then there's a club with thorns."

"Weird," I repeat.

"Club," she points out.

"A mace actually," Lucas inserts. "With spikes."

Eloise pauses, leans forward, and then narrows her eyes. "A mace? Why does it feel alive?"

Her psychic abilities go much deeper than just spiritual reading. She's also an empath and extremely sensitive to auras and energy. Trying to lie to her as a teenager was a bitch. Hence, why I never tried more than once.

"It's sentient," Lucas replies. "Think a guardian inside of a weapon."

Stunned, Eloise glances at me.

I shrug. "Apparently, that's what you get when you channel an archdemon, and then have a one-night stand with a fallen angel."

Eloise shakes her head. "You are *so* my kid."

A sharp laugh escapes me, mainly because I did not expect that response.

"Let's eat," I suggest.

We barely make it through the meal when my chair slides backward away from the table, completely on its own. Blood trickles out of my nose, and my hand flies to my face to staunch a gush that never comes.

Eloise cries out.

For once, Lucas doesn't rush to help. He simply turns his chair, leans his elbows on his knees, and watches me.

I'm trying to breathe, not because I can't, but because I feel swollen, my body full of something extremely dark and terrifying. Like a doll stuffed with super-charged cotton.

"He can't do it," Lucas says.

Breathing through the panic crippling me, I look at him. "Can't do what?"

"Possess you." He stares, amazed. "He keeps trying. I can feel it. He's drawing on your energy, but he's not *entering* you."

"I'd say that sounds like a dirty joke, but," nausea slams into me, "this really hurts."

Lucas finally comes to me, kneels, and touches my chin. "You're not going to throw up."

Bile rises in my throat, metallic and hot, and I swallow past it. "Those are pretty words—"

"Fight it, Harper." He drops his hand.

I clutch my stomach and double over. "Fight it," I repeat. *You're not going to throw up.*

Inside my head, I start to scream, loud and shrill. Over and over again. The sound chases back the nausea.

My hands start to shake. Even pressed against my stomach, I can feel the tremors.

I lift them.

Aunt Eloise gasps. "Paper."

Rushing into her bedroom, she returns with pencils and a notepad. I shake my head, even as my chair slides back toward the table. Once again, all on its own.

"I can't do this," I insist.

Lucas joins me. "Yes, you can. Use your gifts. If a lesser demon tries to interfere, I've got you. There's not a damn thing they can do if I'm here."

Pushing the food aside, Eloise places the notebook and pencils in front of me, the cover flipped open.

"Aunt Eloise," I beg.

My hands are shaking so violently now, they hurt.

"It's okay," she promises, even though I can tell by the waver in her voice, she's not sure it is.

As soon as I lift my hand, it flies to the pencils. Gripping one of them, my fingers jerk to the notebook, and I feel my eyes rolling up inside of my head.

My world goes dark.

When I come to, Lucas is leaning over the table, furrows marring his forehead.

Beneath my fingers are the words, *You can't protect her, Luke. She's mine. Power. Time to suffer.*

Dropping the pencil, my hands fly to my throat, but there's no choking sensation like there was in Jeanine Turner's office. "Luke?" I rasp.

Lucas stares at the message. Small drops of blood are smeared over the ink. "Levi and I have known each other for a very, very long time." It's the only explanation he gives for the nickname.

"You can't protect her? She's mine?" Eloise massages her forehead. "I don't understand. This isn't about Harper, *is* it?"

Lucas touches the notebook. "We're talking about an archdemon who has had a very long time to build a grudge and make plans. I'm sure he has multiple agendas." Picking up one of the pencils, he taps it against the sheet. "Will you write for me again, Harper?"

My blood runs cold. "Lucas . . ."

Coming up behind me, he cages me in with his arms, the pencil in his fingers goading me. "Trust me. Write. Except this time, I want you to *think* about a name. Meri. She's a demon of fate in the underworld and an old friend."

"An ex-lover?" I ask, immediately kicking myself for the question and the terse way it comes out.

Lucas's head lowers, his mouth near my ear. "Jealous?" He sounds amused.

"No."

His breath whispers against my skin. "Not an ex-lover. I've dabbled with demons, but not this one. She's too prickly." He chuckles. "No one wants to tangle with a demon of fate." Holding out the pencil, he offers it to me. "Meri. Think about her name and ask her about Lucas and Leviathan."

When I don't move, he cups my shoulder with his hand. "Open yourself up, Harper. Take back control of your power."

My back stiffens.

Out of everything he could have said, *this* is what pushes me forward. Because there's nothing I want more than control over something I've been robbed of.

"Are you sure about this?" Eloise asks. She sounds nervous, and that settles it.

She's been robbed, too.

Meri's name echoing through my head, I take the pencil. *Leviathan,* I think. *Lucas.*

The response is immediate.

My hand swerves onto the notebook, the lines that appear surprisingly flowery and feminine.

Well, if it isn't the golden boy himself. Hello, honey.

As crazy as it sounds, joy races through me, the feeling replacing the horrible fatigue I felt when Levi forced my hand. *This* is what I'm supposed to do. This is what Eloise does for others, channeling spirits and the deceased for her customers. I may be channeling a demon, but

I feel in control. Me. In control. I hope, anyway, and if I'm not, I don't want to know, because this feels good.

Lucas snorts. "Give me the rundown, Meri," he demands aloud.

My hand scribbles. *No sweet nothings? No, "It's been a long time and I miss you, Meri?"*

"I want answers," Lucas replies.

The pencil pauses, and then, *You imprison an archdemon with little more than a symbol of water and you expect that to hold?*

Lucas's hand fists on the table. "That was before my fall. I've learned a lot about your world since then. Firsthand. Even so, the symbol was strong enough."

I swear I hear Meri laugh in my head. *You are so cute, angel. The symbol has crumbled. The only thing keeping him there now is weakness. It only takes two things for a demon like him to rise.*

"Blood and energy," Lucas murmurs.

If you know, why contact me?

"Don't play games with me, Meri. He has secrets, and you're in a position to know that. You owe me. Remember those souls you let escape into—"

My elbow shoots out, catching Lucas just under the ribs. He grins.

The pencil scratches. *I'm disappointed in you. Why bring up old wounds?*

"The information, Meri," Lucas prompts.

Look to your psychic. Levi has been planning this since her birth. He has allies. Do you not feel the woman? Curses. Black magic. Blood. Power. Now, our debt is repaid. Leave me.

I lose my grip on the pencil, and it falls onto the table, bouncing off of the notebook before rolling onto the floor. My body sags in the chair.

Eloise slides a steaming cup of tea in front of me. "Green tea with ginseng." She'd been busy while I was transcribing. "For energy. Sessions take a lot out of the messenger. I'm proud of you, Harper."

Tears threaten to choke me.

Lucas tugs the notebook toward him. "Tell me about your parents again," he says.

Eloise answers for me. "There isn't much to know. A psychic and a mortal fell in love, fought for years to have a baby together, and then went to a black arts practitioner for help when the Court refused to do dark magic to save the child. Surely, you don't need it said aloud when you can hear it in our thoughts."

He glances at me. "I can't hear it in hers. There is nothing except silence in Harper's head."

Eloise looks at me. I sip the tea.

"I think we need to try this again," Lucas suggests.

Eloise recoils. "What? Do you know what channeling does to a person?"

"Unless I'm missing my guess, it just gave your niece a second wind."

He's right. Unlike the times I'd been controlled in the past and unlike the times Levi had used me, this felt different. Empowering. I sag in the chair not because I'm tired, but because I'm relieved.

Is it because I called on the demon rather than the demon calling on me?

"Harper?" Aunt Eloise asks.

"He's right," I admit. "I feel stronger."

Confusion eats at Eloise's face, leaving gnawed lines of concentration. "You should feel weaker."

Lucas leans toward me, completely focused on my face. "I think you need to try channeling your mother."

I don't know if the whimper that echoes through the room is mine or Eloise's.

CHAPTER 10

"You can't be serious," Eloise cries. "No. Absolutely not."

I'm frozen.

I never knew my mother. She is a myth, this idea I've built up like a wall inside of my head.

She is memories I created for myself from nothing. She is warm arms that never actually held me. She is brave words I never got a chance to hear. She is loud, angry lectures I never got the chance to endure.

Memories built out of imagination.

Okay, I tell myself. Because giving myself permission first somehow makes it easier to say it out loud.

"Why would you even ask this of her?" Eloise cries. Her question opens into a long string of rants, protests, and objections, and even though I hear what she's saying, it's like white noise behind louder thoughts. I'm focused on only one word.

"Okay." My voice isn't loud when I say it, but it has the power to quiet the room.

After a long moment of silence, Eloise reaches for me, aghast. "Harper, you don't have to do this. It's not the same, channeling family. It's," she closes her eyes, and then opens them again, "It's just not the same. You have no idea."

The thing is, I've already given myself permission to be okay with this. Because, in the grander scheme of things, my feelings are small compared to the knowledge we need.

My head rises, my eyes finding the angel looming above me. "Okay." Lucas smiles. "Okay," he replies. He touches my face, and I'm prepared for him to back away, my mind and body primed to turn to the table and face my fears, when he suddenly slides his hand into my hair, startling me. His eyes darken, his fingers tangling with the strands. Lifting my face, he lowers his head, takes a moment to search my gaze, and then kisses me. Deeply. Briefly.

He tastes like spring feels.

"For being brave," he says when he pulls back.

The kiss stuns my aunt into silence. In truth, it does the same for me, not because I don't know what it's like to kiss Lucas, but because I sense something in the way he kissed me. Understanding, maybe?

Something feels different when I turn back to the table.

Flipping to a new page in the notebook, I reach for another pencil, mentally steeling myself against the destruction of something momentous. My mother is a fairy tale I created.

Memories built out of imagination. A house of cards dangerously close to toppling.

I inhale through my nose, the breath deep and fortifying. *Mom,* I call, and when I get no immediate response, I add, *Karen Sinclair.*

The house of cards crumbles.

The pencil slides across the page. *Harpists harp harping. My Harper.*

The words are everything I hoped for and everything I feared. Tears cloud my vision, and even though I want to walk away from this, I maintain my grip on the pencil. Unlike Lucas with the demon of fate, I don't talk to my mother out loud. I do it in my head. I'm not brave enough to share everything. Not yet.

Why did you do it? I ask Mom.

The pencil leaves loops and elegant word slopes on the page. A handwriting as beautiful on paper as she is in my head.

My dear child. My hopes. My dreams, she replies.

I am her everything.

Words I've thought a million times over the years, but never had the courage to say, flow out into the spirit realm, slow and unsure. *I shouldn't have been born, Mom.*

Meant to be, she protests. *You were meant to be.*

She's wrong. I was *made* to be.

Mom! I cry in my head, the wail loud and full of frustration. I'm not even sure why I say it. Maybe it's because I haven't had the opportunity to do it before, to wail with annoying repetition the way I know I would have done had she lived. *Mom. Mom. Mom.*

My pencil suddenly races over the paper, frenzied and all over the place. *She's coming,* Mom says. *She will come. He owns her. She will come, and you will destroy her. You will break your curse. A curse that was never a curse. A moment that was never bad. A childhood that was robbed too soon.*

She's not making any sense.

My curse? I ask.

Harpists harp harping. Angels airily dancing. On clouds, casting glances. Their eyes glowing brightly. Guarding. Guiding. And that's how you got your name. So says me.

She's a madwoman, even in death. I quit fighting the tears, and they slip unchecked down my cheeks. Quiet and deadly. *I killed you, Mother.*

There, I admitted it. Long before I was even born, I destroyed her mentally. Her need to have me was much stronger than her mind.

The pencil stiffens, as if angry, before scratching out, *No, you gave me purpose. She killed me, but she gave you what you needed to live. She's coming. Written in the stars.*

I can't make sense of anything she's saying, but I can feel my connection with her growing weaker, and out of desperation, I say the one thing I've been waiting a long time to tell her. "I'm sorry."

This time, I say it out loud.

Harpists harp harping. Angels airily dancing. On clouds, casting glances. Their eyes glowing brightly. Guarding. Guiding. And that's how you got your name. So says me. The pencil falls.

My eyes fall shut with it, closing out the world, my imagination trying desperately to rebuild the house of cards I had held onto so tightly all of these years.

"You shouldn't have asked her to do that," Eloise says shortly to Lucas.

She's wrong.

Despite losing the innocent childhood fairy tale I'd conjured up for myself, I am glad I connected with my mother. It let me face the grief I haven't been able to let go of until now.

I feel more confident. Strong.

My eyes reopen. Mom's words glare up at me from the notebook, and I just *know*. Flipping from Meri's words to my mother's, my mind pieces together what was left unsaid. "The woman who cursed our family is a demon. Not a witch. A demon."

Aunt Eloise places a hand on the table, bracing herself, and the temptation to go to her is strong. This isn't any easier on her than it is on me.

"Harper." Tugging me out of the chair, Lucas pulls me into his embrace, and I know by the way he hugs me that he senses my need to hug my aunt.

He's giving me what I can't give her right now.

"The woman is a demon," I repeat.

Lucas's arms tighten around me. "It makes sense. Meri's information. Your mother's words. The other demon I've been feeling . . . she's the sorceress your parents sought out. Meri's right. Levi has had this planned for a long time." Pulling back, he looks down into my face. "The demoness your parents went to must have felt your father's psychic powers and your psychic potential. If Levi had already reached out to her, she would have been looking for a way to help him break free. Your family would have been a breath of fresh air for her."

"Why?" Eloise asks, her voice rough with emotion. "Why would she help an archdemon?"

Lucas glances at her. "Because, while there are good demons in this world—somewhat—there are others who prefer the evil they were born from. In the underworld, there is no greater position than becoming an archdemon. To achieve it, you fight your way to the top, you make alliances with more powerful demons, and if you are a lesser demon, you find a way into an archdemon's good graces."

It all makes sense. The message Levi sent. His need to leave the Infernum. His vendetta against Lucas. My issues with writing.

The theory Lucas had earlier about Levi using me as a sacrificial altar rears its ugly head, and I gasp when a horrible thought suddenly occurs to me.

If the demoness used me as a way to open a connection with Levi, then . . . "No!"

My eyes widen in horror. "The man I gave the message to when I was a child . . ." The words trail off because they are too terrible to say out loud.

My aunt inhales, and I know she's thinking it, too, which means Lucas must know. He would see it in her thoughts.

Blood and energy.

No!

Fisting my hands in Lucas's shirt, I peer up at him, desperate. "Please tell me I didn't sacrifice him to Levi. Please. You know these kinds of things, right? You know how they work. Please, please tell me I didn't."

The angel can't meet my gaze. "You wouldn't have known. You were a child, Harper."

I back away from him, horrified. "No, please tell me he wouldn't." My words break on horrible sobs. "He wouldn't use a child for something like that, would he?"

"He's an archdemon desperate to escape a prison. A sacrifice made in his name would weaken the gateway. The fact that you went so long avoiding your gift afterward held him in check. Until now."

Hope flares, and I grasp at it. "But I did write. In school. At first."

Lucas frowns. "He would have been weaker then, and you had the Court's help. You didn't write completely exposed without any protection again until recently."

"Oh, my God!" I stumble across the room until the living room wall stops me. My body slides down it. "No!" I say the word over and over again, and still it's not enough. It's unforgiveable.

My gaze, clouded by grief and horror, finds Lucas. "How? How did Levi kill him?"

"Ask your aunt."

I can't breathe. My eyes fly to Aunt Eloise's grief-stricken face. Her expression says more than words ever could, and still I ask, "What? How?"

She steps toward me, her hand out, placating. "Harper, we didn't tell you because we thought it was best. We—"

"Tell me what?"

Her eyes fall shut, the lids squeezing a tear down her cheek. "The man . . . they ruled it a suicide, but they found the message you gave him stuffed inside of his mouth. He—"

"Stop," I sob. I don't want to know any more. I can't breathe. It's completely impossible to breathe. I am not a coward for not wanting to know. I am *not* a coward.

I don't need to know the details. What I need is to keep my sanity. Some secrets are better left with the Court and its members. How many secrets are they hiding for others in the town? How many of us are they protecting? How many of us are they trying to save?

The importance of Havenwood Falls—what this place means to me —is bigger than any word. This town is my mother. This town is the fairy tale my mother couldn't be. They kept me safe, even when I couldn't always keep myself or others safe.

My head hangs.

"Harper," my aunt pleads.

I was a child. I have to keep reminding myself of that. I have to.

A steely determination settles over me, and when I lift my face, I know my eyes are full of fire and hatred. The archdemon and his lackey will be destroyed. I'll make sure of it.

When I look at Lucas, my gaze locking with his stormy eyes, I think I know what it's like to live where he does. In the gray area among blurred lines.

CHAPTER 11

"We have a visitor," Lucas says.

A few minutes later, a series of knocks sounds on the shop door.

Aunt Eloise rushes upstairs. Voices murmur. Footsteps sound on the stairs.

Saundra Beaumont is the first to appear, Eloise fast on her heels.

Serious brown eyes scope out the room before settling on Lucas. "Our wards were tripped. According to some of the shifters, it's a demon. A female. I'm guessing yours." Saundra's gaze swings my way, her eyes softening when she sees me sitting on the floor, my face swollen from tears. "Oh, Harper."

Her eyes return to Lucas. "She's stirring up the shifters, and I've had calls from some of the demons in town who've sensed her, too. They're about as happy about this as we are. They've found peace here in Havenwood Falls, and I'm not letting an asshole among their kind ruin it. We're all prepared to stop her. What's it going to be, angel?"

"She won't come into town," Lucas replies confidently, his gaze finding me. "She wants Harper, and I want Levi." Gesturing at me, he adds, "We'll take this into the mountains."

"Don't be stubborn, angel. Your arrogance gets you nothing when dealing with evil. You're going to need some help."

"Only if it gets desperate. This is my fight. And hers."

She's obviously not happy with Lucas's response, but there's a strange respectful relationship between the witch and the angel, and I don't know if it's because they knew each other before this incident or if they'd heard about each other through supernatural channels.

"We'll be ready to step in," Saundra warns, turning, her gaze falling on the table. On Desi. She freezes, her eyes widening. "I thought I sensed something. What the hell is that?"

"A weapon," Lucas answers, grinning.

Sighing, Saundra presses a hand to her chest. "I think it's better I don't ask. Especially today. No one has ever accused this town of being dull." She gives Lucas a firm look. "If that thing does more than stay a bat, you better get it registered with the Court."

"It's a mace," he corrects.

"Hmm." With one final bewildered look, Saundra rushes up the stairs.

I can't quit staring at my aunt's apartment. At the wild walls and strange dolls. I hear things—my aunt talking with Saundra in the shop, Lucas moving around the room upstairs, and the heat blasting from my aunt's furnace—but my scope of the world has narrowed to me and the pictures on the wall.

I find myself among the painted sketches.

"Harper?"

Lucas is talking to me, but I can't look at him. My body feels like a ship caught on rough seas, in danger of capsizing.

My portrait—a rendition of me at least ten years younger than I am now—frowns at me on the wall, the eyes blinking. Around it, the other pictures come to life. Some of them reach for me. Others dance.

I am hallucinating.

"Harper."

My body catches fire.

Voices consume me.

Someone screams, the sound shrill and desperate, the wild wail full of pain and hopelessness. Grief and anguish.

The screams belong to me.

"All right," I hear Lucas say, "I'm going to need your help after all. The demon is already calling on Levi. We've got to move fast."

Someone looms over me. Saundra, maybe, but she doesn't look like Saundra. She looks like a watercolor version of herself, all fuzzy and blurred around the edges.

I taste blood in my mouth.

Pain lances through my stomach.

Someone lifts me. "It's going to be okay," Lucas whispers against my ear.

I wonder if he can promise me that. I wonder if sacrifices are ever meant to be okay. I wonder if *I* was ever meant to be okay.

My world slips away into nothingness.

CHAPTER 12

I am lost to a world of dreams.

"*I'VE BEEN WAITING a long time for you," a deep voice says.*

Even though I've never heard his voice, I know who it is, and I hate him. Levi.

A forked tongue dances in front of my face. "Do you feel it?" Levi asks. "Power." He inhales. "Ah, it feels good."

A serpent large enough to be a dragon slithers into view. Straight out of darkness. There is only him and a black backdrop.

"We finally meet, Harper Sinclair."

"Where am I?" I ask.

"Dreams," he answers. "The horror of the Infernum without actually being here. Maddeningly dark, isn't it?"

There's nowhere to go. Nowhere to hide. Only blackness.

"Why?"

He laughs, circling me, his tongue hissing. "Because you have the power to pull me free."

"I don't," I protest. "My family . . . we don't have that kind of power."

"You do." He sounds so sure of himself.

Anger wells up inside of me, and I spin, trying my best to keep up with him as he moves. Faster and faster we go.

"You made me do terrible things," I call out, my voice shaking. I have a bad habit of crying when I'm angry.

"You could be so much more than what you are, Harper," Levi tells me. He stops so abruptly, I almost fall into him, his large, reptilian eyes glowing red. He has silver scales, and they shine even though there's no light to make them glow. "You were born from darkness. Just like the demons here. A human born to the underworld. Your soul for power," he offers. "Give me your humanity, and you'll never feel pain again. You'll never know it."

"Harper."

Somewhere beyond the darkness, someone calls my name.

Levi hisses, his fangs flashing. "Choose!" he yells, all patience gone.

"You will die," I tell him, my voice frosty. "For what you've done to that man when I was small. For what you've done to people. You will die."

I suddenly wish I knew the man I'd given the message to. What his name was and whether or not he had a family. Maybe it's better he stays unknown to me, but there is power in knowing a name. A power that lets people put things to rest, and I want to put him to rest. I need to put him to rest.

"You will die," I promise.

Levi's eyes glow. "You would have been magnificent."

Fangs dripping, he lunges for me.

I FALL INTO ANOTHER DREAM.

I AM INSIDE A TENT. Other than a circle of lit candles, an athame, and a snake—a large dark boa constrictor—there is nothing in the space except a cloaked elderly woman sitting cross-legged in the center of the candles. The snake slithers around her, easing his body through her legs and over her clothes. Squeezing her. Loving her.

Long, stringy silver hair surrounds a face as craggy as a mountain. The woman's eyes are closed.

It's hot inside the space, the air so thick and heavy, it's hard to breathe. I catch a whiff of stagnant mud and sulfur.

A rustling at the tent's entrance draws my attention.

Two figures duck inside.

I gasp. My parents.

The woman's eyes pop open. "Why have you come to me?"

My mother—a woman I've only seen in pictures—steps forward. Her stomach is swollen, her long brown hair pulled protectively around her shoulders, her green eyes glowing. She looks too young to be my mother. She looks like me. I look like her.

My dad is a study in opposites. Auburn hair. Brown eyes. Slender and athletic. A pair of glasses sits perched on his nose, the spectacles softening a face that would otherwise be rugged.

"We need help," my mother pleads.

The woman waves at her candle-lit circle, and my parents join her. Heads bent, they whisper frantic words I'm not meant to hear.

"Stop!" I beg them. "She's going to hurt you."

I am nothing and no one.

The elderly woman lifts the athame, pulls the ceremonial knife free from its sheath, and places it against my mother's stomach.

I can't look.

I can't look away.

Lifting my mother's shirt, the woman grins, baring rotten teeth and gums glistening with spittle.

"Don't!" I beg.

She plunges the athame into my mother's pregnant belly.

If she screams, it's lost to me.

"Help me," I cry.

CHAPTER 13

"Y ou've got to quit thrashing, Harper," Lucas murmurs. I wake inside of his arms on top of the mountains, a waxing crescent moon hanging among a backdrop of tiny sequins. Air puffs from my lungs into a dark sky, the world below white and brilliant.

"What happened?" I am cold. So very, very cold.

Setting me down, Lucas pulls my coat tighter, his body supporting mine when I stumble, my legs weak. "Gillian did a ritual on the mountain."

"Gillian?"

He frowns. "That's the name of the demoness your parents approached. She moves fast. By the time the Court realized she was here and Saundra got to us, she was already in a trance and drawing blood. She needed your energy to pull Levi from the Infernum." He lifts my shirt, and even though I don't see any claw marks, I know they were there. I felt the pain inside my aunt's apartment.

"Did the Court send someone to stop her?"

"A few shifters came, mainly to keep an eye on her. We didn't want to stop her. We needed her to finish it. Levi needs to be destroyed before he can cause any more danger here or anywhere." Slipping his arm around my waist, he assists me through the snow and up onto a ridge. Pine trees look like looming monsters in the night, their angry shadows prowling on wind and frozen ground.

There, sitting comfortably among the white powder, is a young woman. Midnight hair flows down her back, the strands framing a pale face, red lips, and eyes as black as her hair. She's covered in dark leather, from the pants encasing her slender legs to the crop top wrapping her chest. Evidently, the cold doesn't bother her.

Glancing up, she grins, her eyes taking on a red hue. "It's about time you joined me," she greets.

"You're not her," I say.

Gillian looks nothing like the woman I saw in the dream. She looks nothing like the woman who plunged a dagger through my mother's pregnant belly.

"Glamours are beautiful things," she replies. "I was a lot more repugnant when I stole you from your parents."

Anger writhes like a flame inside of me. She senses it, her gaze lifting to mine.

"Oh my, you are precious." Standing, the demon saunters toward us, confidence lending an exaggerated sway to her hips. "Do you know how long I've waited to see how you would turn out?"

Pausing a short distance away, she studies me. "I'm not disappointed. What a beautiful creation I've made." She glances at Lucas. "You're too late. I've already summoned him."

"No," Lucas replies, surprising her. "I am just in time." He steps toward her. "You see, I don't play games. I was flying with angels and fighting with demons long before you ever blinked into existence." Lucas's gaze searches the ridge. "Come to me, Levi. You called. This time, I won't send you back to the Infernum. I will destroy you."

From the edge of the woods, the massive silver serpent from my dream slithers into view, his scales flashing as he moves. The only thing human about him are two arms protruding from his reptilian frame.

His forked tongue tastes the air, his red eyes finding me. "It's a pity you wouldn't offer me your soul."

"What did you do to me?" I ask, and I don't mean the ritual Gillian performed or the dreams I had because of it. We've known since the first mark appeared on my skin that Levi planned to use my psychic energy to manifest into the mortal world.

I mean other things. I mean dark things. I mean plunging a knife into my mother's belly kind of things.

Levi lunges for me, fangs glistening, so fast I don't have any time to react.

Lucas blurs past me, his hand catching the beast by the neck, his body suddenly glowing, a golden light surrounding him. Massive wings spill out of his back. Six of them altogether. All of them on fire. His pupils lighten, his angry eyes going colorless, white and terrifying.

"This is between you and me, demon," Lucas growls.

He throws Levi. The serpent rolls in the snow, his body coiling.

Hissing, Levi rights himself, his snake-like form growing in the night. Fire shoots out of his mouth. "The audacity you have is astounding. You have friends among my kind, and yet you felt the need to lock me away. You will pay for that."

"I could have killed you, Levi. I showed too much mercy by letting you live." From somewhere I can't see, Lucas produces a long, flaming sword, a feral grin spreading across his face. "Let's dance."

An object whizzes past me, and I barely have time to sidestep it when Desi appears, the mace slamming into Gillian's surprised face.

I shriek, taken aback.

"Never turn your back on a battlefield," Desi sings.

Gillian came for me while the demon and the fallen angel were fighting, my distraction a weakness I can't afford.

I am way out of my league. They all move too fast for me, they're stronger, and they have more power. I am a puppet being forced to join a battle I don't know how to win.

Gillian stumbles backward, her hand swiping at her face. Blood beads up from a gash on her forehead, the crimson fluid smearing where she's touched it.

Furiously, she kicks at the mace, and it rushes away from her in the snow, leaving a trail of turned up white powder. "Damn you, Destroyer," she hisses.

Her gaze finds mine, and I know, even before she sends me flying, that I'm no match for this fight. I'm no match for the massive serpent, flaming wings, and glamour-spelled woman.

I know even before I go flying that I'm going to die.

Power hits me like a brick wall, the force of it throwing me into the air before shoving me into the snow, the weight of it stealing my breath and pressing me into the ground.

A howl rises from the forest, and a wolf emerges from the woods.

Ric Kasun. Even from a distance, I know it's him. Behind him, Saundra Beaumont steps free of the trees, her face angry. Other faces emerge with them, but my vision blurs as I struggle to breathe.

Gillian ignores them, her laughter loud on the echoing ridge as she approaches me.

Desi rushes through the snow, plowing a line directly under the power shield holding me captive, and a bright light flares. Sparks rain down around us, and I cover my head. The power's weight no longer suffocates me.

"Remember where you came from," the mace growls.

Something lands in the snow beyond our small circle, the force of it shaking the ground. Fire flames outward, so bright I have to look away, and I know by the golden hue coating the ground that it's Lucas.

Shaking snow off of himself, the fallen angel rises, a glorious sight, the size and breadth of him too much for human eyes. He's discarded his shirt, his fiery wings coating his skin in undulating flames.

As a bare-chested Seraph in full battle mode, Lucas is magnificent.

He launches himself into the sky, his blazing wings barely moving as he glides up, his face fierce when he roars, the sound filling the mountains. It sounds like thunder in the night, and I wonder if that's how the Court will tell this story one day.

The night when thunder fought thunder in the mountains.

I stumble to my feet.

"Remember what you are!" Desi yells.

Gillian stalks me, circling me like a predator.

What am I?

Raising her hand, Gillian clenches her fist. Once again, I fly into the air, my back slamming against the trunk of a bare oak tree, before being dragged up the rough bark.

Pain rips through me, and even though I try not to scream, it comes out anyway.

Desi soars into the scene, flitting from side to side like an annoying house fly before swiping at the demon's feet and knocking her onto the ground.

My back slides down the tree.

Snarling, Gillian grabs the mace and throws it into the night, and I watch, horrified, as it sails over the side of the mountain.

When she turns back to look at me, Gillian's eyes are the color of blood. "Pledge your soul to Levi and this ends, Harper. All of it."

"What did you do to my mother?" I ask, losing sight of the fight in the sky.

Gillian smiles. "I gave her what she wanted. I sank my blade into her womb, destroying what was killing you, before using my power to give you new life. You should thank me. You are here because of me."

"I lost everything because of you."

"I could take away your pain," she offers. "Pledge your soul to Levi and this ends."

Burning heat sears my back from the scrapes and gashes left behind by the tree, and I grit my teeth against the hurt. "I'd rather die," I finally manage.

Gillian marches toward me, a ball of red flame forming in her hands. "Maybe you'd rather die, but would you trade your soul for your angel's?"

Stepping aside, she gestures at the heavens, the red blaze dancing in her palm.

Terror engulfs me.

In the night, a great firestorm appears in the sky. It's a conflagration of unnatural light hanging unchecked in the atmosphere. Blue and red sparks shoot up and down a tower of orange flames like fireworks.

Lucas hovers beneath it, his colorless gaze on the fire. He doesn't look afraid, but I know by the gleeful grin on Levi's face and the way the archdemon circles in the air above Lucas, that the blaze between them is Lucas's weakness.

Sailing to the side, Lucas avoids the flames, his fiery sword swinging. It connects with Levi's tail, and the beast roars.

The firestorm barrels toward Lucas.

Gillian smiles. "That's my cue."

In a blur, she's closed the distance between us, her breath on my face, her fingers circling my neck. A familiar athame materializes in her free hand, and she places the point against my stomach.

Howls rip the air.

Behind Gillian, wolves gather, Ric Kasun leading the pack. Flanking him are his sons, Conall and Tate Kasun. Even in wolf form, I can tell them apart. By spending most of my days hiking or camping in the mountains and woods, I have developed a respectful relationship with the shifters in Havenwood Falls. We've barely talked in the years I've known them, but I've learned that shifters don't always need words. They protect me from a distance, and I don't take any pictures of them.

Members of the Luna Coven gather with the wolves. Roman Bishop, a lean, tall warlock and a member of the coven's High Council, watches with narrowed eyes and crossed arms. Flanking him are Ronya Augustine and Addie Beaumont. Both are witches. Addie is the closest to my age, and she nods at me, her brown eyes staring from behind black-framed glasses. She is the only girl who attempted to spend time with me in high school. Even though she says nothing now, her gaze yells, "Fight, Harper!"

Saundra Beaumont stands before them all, her gaze on me. There's something violent and powerful about the way she looks at me.

Lifting her hand, she shakes her head at the wolves and the witches, and I know she's ordering everyone not to interfere. I don't know if she has that much faith in me and Lucas or if she's just biding her time.

Remember what you are.

Gillian chants against my ear, the words foreign, and even though I don't understand what she's saying, I know when I see the black hole that opens in the air above us what she's doing.

She's opening a portal to the Infernum.

In the air, fire beats down on Lucas. He doesn't scream, but I know by the look on his face that the pain is agonizing.

He falls to the ground. Dead silence fills the area.

Struggling, I cry out, the sound strangled by Gillian's grip. He has to be okay.

Lucas's head rises in the snow, his gaze meeting mine across the distance, his eyes full of fury when he sees Gillian's hand wrapped around my neck.

Even wounded, he is mighty.

In a blink, he has Gillian in the snow, his flaming sword hovering above her head.

Remember what you are.

Growling, Desi suddenly appears, the mace gliding through the snow toward Lucas, no worse the wear for his trip over the side of the mountain.

My gaze falls on Lucas's back. One side of his six wings is badly damaged, an unnatural blue-tinted burn coating the surface beneath

Lucas's celestial fire. Flames that can scorch an angel already ablaze is an eerie sight, and I realize it's a different kind of burn. An injury no earthly creature can define.

Hesitantly, I step forward, the pull of the wounds on my back making me grimace. "Lucas." He looks at me, and I reach for him. When he doesn't stop me, I run my hand down his good wing. Even though the wings are on fire, the flames don't sear my skin. It's a cool heat, and I realize it feels exactly like his hands felt when he healed me.

My fingers slide to the damaged section, and he hisses.

Above us, the black hole widens. Levi laughs, his serpentine body lowering in the night.

Lucas reaches back, produces three clear vials hidden somewhere in his wings, and pops off the tops. Before Levi even touches the ground, Lucas downs them all.

My eyes widen. I know those vials. My aunt sells them in her shop. "What the hell?" I gasp.

Lucas glances at me and winks.

Holy water. He's just downed three small bottles of holy water.

"I thought—"

"It does," Lucas answers, cutting me off.

The black hole above us shifts, sliding from the air above to the ground below. If I wasn't so unnerved by the portal and the place I know it leads to, I would have found the way it moved wicked cool.

Levi slithers from the sky to the ground, his fangs dripping, the fire that hurt Lucas gathered before him. He doesn't touch it, but he's able to manipulate it.

My eyes are drawn to the way it burns, the inferno dancing on the night air as if it's inside a fireplace rather than out in the open with no wood to fuel it.

The blaze throws streaks of light over my face.

"Brilliant, isn't it?" Levi asks. He leans forward, and I stumble back. "Holy fire. I brought it with me from the Infernum. It's one of the few weaknesses Seraphs have. Ironic, isn't it? Considering Seraphs are made of fire." He sneers. "Then again, the angel trapped me with water, and I was born from the waters of hell. What bears us is often our greatest enemy."

His words pummel me, and I hide the gasp that almost escapes my mouth.

Remember what you are.

What bears us is often our greatest enemy.

You were born from darkness. Just like the demons. A human born to the underworld.

My gaze flies to Gillian, the memory of her driving an athame into my mother's belly like a nail hammered into my subconscious.

Remember what you are.

There's a reason Lucas can't hear my thoughts.

Levi roars, shoving the holy fire at us. We scream, shielding our eyes. My body instinctively falls to the ground, but even though the fire covers me, it doesn't burn. Like everything else, it feels cool.

Not all of us are immune.

Lucas stumbles out of the blaze, his body covered in blue-tinted burns. The fire suddenly flares, and then vanishes, revealing a circling Levi as he edges Lucas closer and closer to the Infernum portal.

Crying out, I lunge for them, but Gillian grabs me by the ankle, dragging me backward, her hands clawing at me.

"You're mine!" she growls. Flipping me over, she crawls up my body, her fingers sliding up my sides. I feel more than see the claws that she digs into me.

Claws? Was she the one who left the marks on me? Not Levi. Was I simply a part of a ritual she and Levi were doing together? He bled prisoners. She used me as an altar, opening me up to bleed what he killed.

Her face transforms, her smooth pale skin aging before my eyes until she's the elderly woman from my nightmare.

Remember what you are.

My fingers curl into the snow. The cold is unbearable, but adrenaline pumps through my veins, heating limbs that would have given up already under normal circumstances.

"I am psychic," I say through gritted teeth.

She laughs.

"I am a spiritual writer," I continue.

My fingers begin to move in the snow, writing words I cannot see, power rushing into the ground. Shadows appear over the snow, and even though I am startled by their appearance, I keep writing.

"And I was born of darkness by a demoness who tied my psychic abilities to demons and the Infernum," I finish.

Lucas could never hear my thoughts because the Infernum is the one place a Seraph cannot enter unless he's imprisoned there.

I know even before the shadows descend on Gillian that I've won. Darkness cloaks her, invisible hands clawing at her skin, causing the same kind of wounds she and Levi had caused on me. She screams, and the shadows drag her away, pulling her toward the Infernum.

These shadows aren't prisoners. They're something else.

"Levi!" she screams.

He doesn't pay her any attention. He's too focused on Lucas.

"Wait!" I tell the shadows, my fingers still digging in the snow. Word after word after word. "Bring her to me."

Gillian slams into the ground before me.

I don't know what I'm doing. I don't even know how I'm doing it. All I know is that the only way to close the portal is to take out the woman who opened it. My chest burns, and it isn't that I'm sad. It's that death has become too much a part of me, and I'm afraid of what that means.

Desi slides through the snow toward me. "You've got a lot to learn about what you are, summoner."

What he calls me shocks me, and I stare at him. "Summoner?"

I'm talking to a supercharged baseball bat in the middle of a celestial battle. *This* has become my life.

"The spirits you channel, you can control them," Desi replies.

Levi and Lucas face off, and I know by the way Lucas staggers, both from pain and obvious drunkenness, he's in danger of falling into the portal.

"Can I close it?" I ask Desi.

"What?" the mace asks.

"If I kill the demoness, will it close the portal?"

Desi slides closer to me. "I don't know. She used your energy and her blood to open it."

Lucas falters, and even though I know this fight with Levi is his, I rush to him.

He tries sidestepping me and goes down in the snow. "Go," he orders, not unkindly.

"Get ready!" Saundra calls. Wolves and witches circle.

In a blur, Levi shoves me aside, and I slide into the snow, just as the archdemon grabs Lucas by the neck. "Do you know what it's like living inside a place full of so much immense power, and yet you can't touch it? Do you know what it's like being surrounded by beings you can't fight with or destroy? Do you know what it's like existing in darkness?"

Lucas simply stares at him.

Lifting the angel, Levi holds him over the hole to the Infernum.

I scream.

Lucas laughs.

Levi falters, his body coiling, the sudden movement drawing Lucas toward safety. "You have years of unimaginable torture ahead of you, and you laugh?" the archdemon asks angrily.

For one brief moment, I feel pity for Levi. Because, as ridiculous as his anger seems over a little laughter, I understand where it comes from. I harbor the same hatred for Levi and Gillian after what they did to my parents. After what they did to me. After what they did to innocent lives.

Lucas laughs again. "You will never win, Levi. Not when there are towns like Havenwood Falls. Not when there are creatures, gods, and monsters who want to coexist together peacefully."

Levi throws him against the snow, wraps his hands around Lucas's neck, bares his fangs, and strikes.

I don't have time to get to him. No one has time to get to him. Everything happens way too fast.

One moment, Levi's fangs are buried in Lucas's neck. The next, the archdemon is coiled up in the snow, struggling to breathe, his face as badly burned as Lucas's body.

It's the holy water, I think, astounded. That's why Lucas drank it.

Lucas tries to stand and falls. He's way too close to the portal.

I scramble through the snow, searching frantically for the one thing I know will help.

Levi rises, his anger even more palpable than it was before. He lunges.

A blur stops him, and I freeze. In the snow, a figure stands between Lucas and the archdemon determined to imprison him. This figure isn't human, although he looks it. Broad and burly, he is every inch the quintessential mountain man, his face covered in a dark, wiry beard.

I know this man. It's the man I saw the day I went to Jeanine Turner's real estate office. The same man who had been watching me outside Coffee Haven.

"I ought to have known you'd be the reason for all of this fuss in the mountains," the man says, glancing back at Lucas.

I continue my search in the snow.

When my hands close over the athame, I clutch it to me and scurry to the spot where the shadowy creatures I summoned hold down a weakened Gillian.

Standing over her, I lift the dagger.

"Don't," Lucas calls out. His voice is weak, his gaze locking with mine.

Levi uses the moment of distraction to plow through the stranger, knocking him aside before taking Lucas and shoving him into the Infernum.

Anger and grief overwhelm me.

I'm not fast enough to save him, but the stranger is.

The mountain man moves too quickly to be anything other than supernatural. With a roar, he reaches in and catches Lucas by the hand, his muscles bulging.

"I'm not strong enough to keep you for long, you old bastard," the man growls. "You'd better do this fast or you're going to be leaving that archdemon in this town, and I can't have that."

Lucas wastes no time. A bright light flashes, glaring and then receding to reveal Lucas and the other man sprawled out in the snow.

"God, I hate you," Lucas says, only it's *not* Lucas speaking. It's his body, but not his voice. "Do this fast, Seraph."

The mountain man's body rises, and I know by the way he moves that Lucas is inhabiting it. "You've been working out, Elias," the mountain man teases in Lucas's voice.

"Close the portal," Desi tells me.

Resuming my position over Gillian, I stand, the athame poised to strike, my hands shaking. The demoness stares up at me, her gaze wide and unflinching.

"Tell me how to close it," I command.

She glares. "You know how to close it, but I don't think you have the guts to do it."

Gillian is everything I could possibly hate in a demon, but she's right. Protecting myself and outright killing her are two entirely different things.

Blood and energy. She used my blood and my energy to open it.

With a cry, I bring the athame down. The blade slashes my stomach, and I watch as the blood drips to the snow below. Falling to my knees beside the demoness, I begin to write in the white powder, letting power run through my veins, spirits whispering in my head.

The portal begins to close.

A shriek shatters the stillness.

In the night, his broad frame standing over the serpent, the mountain man drives Lucas's flaming sword into Leviathan's heart. The gurgling sound of blood fills the air.

For a long moment, no one moves.

Placing his foot against the archdemon, the man pulls the blade free from Levi's chest, lifts the sword, and slices off the demon's head. Even in the darkness, no one misses the smile on the bearded man's face.

The portal vanishes.

An eerie relieved silence falls over the mountain. Wolves meld into the trees. Saundra nods at the mountain man, glances at me, and then motions at someone in the shadows. Men and women, some of them familiar, hurry onto the ridge. They don't speak when they approach me, their hard eyes on the demoness next to me on the ground.

Running my fingers through the snow, I watch as the shadows vanish. The men and women grab Gillian.

"The Court will take care of her," Saundra tells me from where she stands near the trees. Roman, Ronya, and Addie nod at me. My whole life I've known these people, but I've never seen them in this capacity. As warriors ready to fight if the need arose. Warriors ready to take down an archdemon if Lucas had failed. Warriors willing to die for the town they reside over.

The group sent by Saundra, a petulant but restrained Gillan between them, ducks into the forest. The demoness had been eerily silent near the end, and I wonder if she wishes I had killed her.

Death is too good for some people.

A bright light flashes, and I cover my eyes. When they open again, Lucas struggles to stand, his wings gone, their flaming beauty hidden away wherever wings hide.

The mountain man offers him a hand.

"Thank you, Elias," Lucas says, and I know by the sound of his voice, he's back in his own body.

"How did you do that?" I ask.

The men look at me.

Elias smirks, claps Lucas on the shoulder, and shakes his head. "As the highest order, your boy here can take over the body of any lower caste angel. He was quite the asshole about it years ago."

"I was a misguided youth," Lucas says.

"You're an angel?" I ask Elias.

"A Divine," he replies.

Outside Coffee Haven isn't the first time I've seen Elias around town, although I can't quite place where else we've run into each other. I've kept to myself too much over the years.

Lucas stumbles, and Elias steadies him.

"The both of you could use healing," Elias points out, his gaze falling to my stomach. It's probably a good thing he can't see my back. His eyes slide up, the bright blue depths softening when they fall on my face. "You did well."

I replace Elias at Lucas's side, my eyes holding the mountain man's gaze. "Thank you."

Pulling Lucas's arm over my shoulders, I wince when it slides across the sensitive skin of my back.

Elias studies me. "Can you make it home?"

"I'll get them there," a new voice pipes up, and I have to fight not to laugh when Elias looks down to find Desi at his feet in all of his badass baseball bat glory.

Only Elias surprises me by *not* being surprised. "It's been a long time since I've seen you, Destroyer. Fly safe." He glances over at Lucas. "And if you do stay in town, don't stir up trouble for those of us who like flying under the radar."

"Boring lot, all of you," Lucas grumbles, a teasing glint in his eyes.

Elias glances between us, a knowing look in his eyes, and then vanishes.

Taking some of his weight off of me, Lucas gazes down into my face. "Let's get you home and healed."

"What about you?"

He offers me a secret smile, and I'm tempted to kiss it away. "I've got a really long history of not dying."

In the night before us, Desi begins to vibrate, the mace quivering violently before transforming into the winged lion I first met in the mountains.

He kneels before us and drops his head.

"To home," Lucas says wearily. He assists me up onto the lion's back even with his injuries, and when he climbs up behind me, I don't mind that he leans on me for support.

"We're not going to fall, are we?" I *do* get rattled on occasion, and being on top of a winged lion right before taking off into the sky is more than enough reason to get rattled.

Lucas chuckles. "He's a fast and smooth flyer, but I won't let you fall, Harper."

CHAPTER 14

*I*t's funny to me how some stories end with more questions than there are answers. There was a time when that frustrated me. Now, it makes sense.

My aunt is the queen of strange stories. Most of the audiobooks she suggests I listen to—books I just *have* to read—are crazy, vivid, and full of more symbolism than answers.

Listening to them, I developed a love for philosophy. A love for looking at the world in a completely different way than most. Quite possibly, my curse has something to do with that, too.

Except I'm not sure I was ever truly cursed.

As soon as we land at my cabin, Desi transforms back into the mace, rolls himself up onto my porch, and settles there.

Inside, Lucas, who seems a little stronger than he did on the ridge, carefully peels away my shirt. Unsnapping my bra, he runs his hands over my skin. Cool heat flares beneath his touch as he heals me. From my back to my stomach.

He kisses the side of my neck.

This time, however, isn't about me.

Spinning in his embrace, I push him toward my bathroom. "I'd ask you to have sex with me, so this would be a lot less awkward for you, but we've already done that."

Lucas's lips twitch, his gaze stroking my face, but he doesn't say anything. Maybe he knows my courage only goes so far. If he speaks, I lose it.

I unbutton his pants, tugging them down over his hips before gently shoving him toward the beveled glass door. "Into the shower with you."

Undressing, I step into the space with him. Water blasts, steam rising, and for the first time in hours, I'm not cold.

I can't look at his face because I'm still learning to be more open, to be the kind of person who can meet someone's gaze without looking away.

Focusing on his skin instead, I run my hands over his chest, over muscle and sinew and healing wounds he seems not to feel. They heal too fast, the water turning a dark shade of blue with the unnatural soot as it washes down the drain. Lucas is too much of everything. Too strong. Too inhuman. He's even too much of an angel among angels. Water slips like rain, rivulets forming on his flesh, and I lean forward, my lips replacing my fingers.

His hand slips into my hair.

No words.

Steam, water, skin, and heavy breaths. This is how I will remember not dying. This is how I will remember pain and lust. This is how I will remember the moment when Lucas went from being a stranger to someone I could possibly fall for. If given the time.

I kiss every wound he has on his skin. I can't heal him the same way he heals me, so I give him what I can as he heals himself. Comfort. Friendship. Understanding.

He lifts me in the shower, pressing me against the wall, and even though I start to protest because I know his body is weakened, he fills me.

My hands slide into his hair, and he kisses me.

Who needs words when lips say things that are too awkward to say out loud? Who needs anything except sensation and fulfillment?

I've often wondered why books say the world explodes and stars rain down when an orgasm hits. Now, I know. It's not just the unmistakable pleasure ripping through me that makes stars dance before my eyes. It's the fact that the world really does feel different.

We leave the shower, dry off, and fall into bed.

Together.

Lucas doesn't sleep, but he does close his eyes. I find myself studying him, my gaze slipping from his golden hair to his rugged face and strong body. Even as muscular as he is, there is a sleek gracefulness to him when he moves. Confidence bred from an eternity of fighting.

Opening his eyes, Lucas smiles when he realizes I'm staring. "You really do have a nice home."

He couldn't have said anything more perfect.

"It really is, isn't it?" I reply.

He opens his arms, and I tuck myself into them. "You're making wise, independent choices."

I laugh. "I'm assuming that means you were a wise, first-choice decision of mine."

"The best."

"Long term or short term?" I ask, because it needs to be asked.

Lucas doesn't reply.

"What happened tonight?" I try again. I've puzzled out most of what I've learned. The revelations about who I am. "Shadows came to me, and Desi called me a summoner?"

Lucas turns his head, his gaze running over my face. "Those weren't shadows. Those were ghosts. Specifically, Hell ghosts, which are a little different from earth ghosts but essentially the same." Pulling me tighter against him, he breathes, "A summoner conjures demons and spirits. It's not unlike what psychics do. Except psychics only channel spirits while a summoner *controls* them. Summoners can even conjure lower caste fallen angels, although if you ask them to do your bidding, you may regret it."

I stare at him. "How am . . . I mean, I don't—"

"Gillian was a summoner," Lucas reveals. He runs his fingers down the side of my face. I've noticed he likes touching, and I don't know if it's because he's with me or because he doesn't get enough of it as a Seraph. "By saving your mother's pregnancy, Gillian made you a part of her. You share her gifts." His brows furrow. "And because Gillian was drawing so much on your energy for the ritual to help Levi escape, she created a connection between you and the Infernum. Which is why I can't read all of your thoughts."

My fingers capture his against my face. "I've had dreams. Most of them make sense now, but . . . but there was one . . ." I cringe. "There was one of me on top of a mountain, overlooking the town. A man, who I assumed was Levi, threatened Havenwood Falls. I'm not sure it was Levi now."

Leaning forward, Lucas kisses me gently on the lips, his face close when he answers, "Being a psychic summoner can either be dangerous or powerful. Now that you know, you can learn to control it. Without control, spirits can use you. You don't want that. You have a bright future, Harper. The dream is a warning that this town, because of what it is, is always in danger. That's why you have the Court. That's why having people like you they can call on is so important. You are going to be an asset here."

He smiles. "I have to admit, you confuse me. That takes power. Some of the things that happened to you were Levi. Some were your powers waking up. I have theories, but maybe all Levi needed was your energy and blood and Gillian's ritual. The Court is going to want to register you as a supernatural. Mortal blood flows through your veins, but you have the ability to call on spirits who would serve you. Who would kill for you if you asked."

"And Gillian?" I ask.

"I don't see them letting her live," Lucas replies. Discomfort lines my eyes and face with troubled thoughts, and Lucas leans his forehead against mine. "If it were up to me, *I* wouldn't let her live. Not only did she perform black magic on your mother, but she devised a way and a ritual to help a powerful demon escape a supernatural prison. That's dangerous information."

He pulls back and lifts my chin. "It took me and a legion of angels and demons to take down Levi hundreds of years ago. If I hadn't fought him here straight after he escaped the prison and while his powers were weak, this wouldn't have been an easy fight. Revenge blinded him. He wanted to imprison me in the Infernum, and he didn't have the patience to wait years for his power to grow. Lack of patience has always been Levi's downfall."

His fingers tighten on my chin. "I want you to remember something. I came into this town prepared for the worst because that's what truly great warriors do. It doesn't matter how easy a fight seems, it can always turn. There are too many variables in battle. Be confident, but don't let confidence blind you."

"You're going to leave, aren't you?"

The smile he gives me is sad. "I have a lot more enemies than just

Levi. I am a risk the Court is not going to want to take, and I don't blame them."

My thoughts go immediately to the mountain man on the ridge. "There are other angels here."

"Not my kind. Not with my history."

I start to speak, but he stops me. "If you're going where I think you're going in your head, don't. You just bought your first house. You have a new beginning here. A place where you'll be safe, where you can finally be the psychic you were meant to be. There are people here you may finally be comfortable enough to get to know. People who need your help. Places you should go. Words won't be dangerous for you anymore. Not once you learn how to control them."

"Did you really think I was going to offer to go with you?" I ask, exaggerating the hurt expression I give him. "That's a really high opinion you have of yourself."

He cocks a brow.

"Okay," I smile, "maybe I was going to suggest it, but I don't think I would have meant it. I just hate," my gaze drops, "that there's no chance to see what this could have been. That there's no chance to get to know you."

"You've seen more of what I am outside of being an angel in the past couple of days than I've let anyone else see in a long time."

I look at him, and this time, I make myself hold his gaze. "You remind me of a falling star. Something beautiful I saw fall from the sky, and then *bam*, gone."

He grins, apparently okay with the analogy. "Did I make wishes come true before I left, at least?"

I nod.

He wraps me in his arms, our bodies pressed close. No barriers. Skin to skin. Beating heart against beating heart.

In the still room, he whispers, "Mortals can be falling stars, too."

CHAPTER 15

*W*hen I wake the next day, Lucas is gone, and even though I expected the absence, my heart clenches like a fist inside my chest.

The house is too silent.

After I dress, I make hot chocolate, the smell rich and deep when I lift the cup to my lips. It doesn't permeate the air quite the same way coffee does, the same way my aunt's apartment always smelled in the morning, but the chocolate is my smell. My scent in the morning.

The sun has already risen, leaving the world white and beautiful. Clean. Shadows climb the walls as the sun climbs in the sky, and I watch them over the rim of my cup. They remind me of the night before.

A psychic summoner. Someone who can both channel spirits and use them. My aunt is a conduit for spirits. She allows them to use her body to send messages to others, but she can't control them. I can. Not only can they use me to send messages, I can call them forth and use them to do my bidding. I can use them as an army, although I have no desire to do it.

A mortal supernatural.

I smile into my cup. Maybe Lucas is right. Mortals can be falling stars, too. I don't make sense as a person, but I do make sense as something in between human and make believe.

Maybe I'm the fairy tale I always tried to make my mother.

"Boy, he sure leaves a big empty feeling behind for having been here for such a short time," I tell the silence.

"That's Lucas for you."

I almost drop my cup of cocoa, my gaze flying to the floor. Desi. "What the hell?"

The mace shudders. "He told me to stay here with you until you're stronger."

The cocoa suddenly doesn't seem like a strong enough morning drink. "And how long will that be?"

"I'll know when," he replies cryptically.

"Great." Now I really *do* have a pet baseball bat. A talking one.

Despite my sarcastic tone, my heart melts. Lucas may have left, but he didn't leave me alone.

"You are not allowed to go into town with me," I tell Desi firmly. "There's no way I can explain you and your nasty looking bronze thorns."

"I don't have to be with you. All you have to do is call me. I'll hear you."

Thank God! I'm not sure I have a backpack big enough to hold him in public.

Speaking of public, I may not have gotten more than a sip from the cup Lucas brought me the other day, but I know Coffee Haven makes really good hot cocoa.

It's time to be brave.

CHAPTER 16

*M*y camera bag slung over my shoulder, I exit Coffee Haven onto the streets of Havenwood Falls with a smile on my face and a second cup of hot cocoa in my hands. In a cup with a *logo*. It's the small things.

On the sidewalk, an elderly woman with a walker meanders by in fancy sweatpants and a pair of sneakers. Big glasses cover most of her face, her lips painted a delicious shade of red. Irene Beckett, a retired schoolteacher and the town's biggest gossip. Even though she's a mortal woman, she knows all about the supernaturals in town, and it doesn't faze her a bit. Maybe that's why the Court lets her knowledge slide. Or maybe they're all as afraid of her as I am. There's something acutely honest and intimidating about Irene. As if, despite her age, she'd give anyone a good fight if challenged.

Even now, her head bent close to a lady I don't recognize, but who I *feel* is a supe, her words play on the breeze like naughty children looking to stir up trouble.

"The black bear kingdom has a new queen, and she . . ." Looking up, she lowers her voice, the words trailing into something too soft to hear. Excitement lights up her face, and her volume rises with it. "Oh, and that Xandru," she shakes her head, tsking, "he and Michaela are on the outs again. Tase is ruining yet another thing in that girl's life, but what can you expect from those Rocas?"

Irene catches me looking and shakes her finger at my face. "Don't be staring at me like that, Harper Sinclair. It's not as if you aren't in on the action in this town. I heard all about your little dalliance with an angel. Shame, shame. A one-night stand? What has the youth come to? There's no such thing as committed relationships anymore."

Technically, it was a two-night stand, but I don't correct her.

I smile. "Commitment would give you nothing to talk about, Mrs. Beckett."

She stops dead in her tracks, the tennis balls on the bottom of her walker resting in snow flurries. "Well . . . oh, my. I'll be damned! You just greeted me like a normal human being. Maybe the sexual awakening did you a little good." She grins. "I hear you may be a force to be reckoned with before long."

"I don't know what scares me the most," I reply. "The way you know things so quickly or hearing you talk about sexual awakenings."

She grunts. "I'm old, not dead, child."

With that, she continues past, head bent, whispering furiously once more.

On her heels, a familiar beard-covered face approaches the door, with shoulders hunched up near his ears and hands deep in the pockets of his pullover shirt. He stomps the snow off of his work boots onto the sidewalk, his eyes catching mine. Elias.

He nods.

I nod back.

He starts to brush past me, but then stops, his voice raspy and low when he asks, "He left?"

I swallow past the sudden lump in my throat.

"It's for the best," he tells me. "Especially with his kind. He'll never age, and he'll never die. You'll do both." He glances down at me. "He's marked you, though."

"Marked me?"

Elias smiles a slow smile. "Something angels do to let other angels know someone is under his protection." His gaze swings to the street, and then back to me. "It doesn't mean you're his. It means he will protect you and that other angels are expected to do the same."

I let his words process in my head before suddenly blurting, "You could be a friend, right? My friend."

Elias raises his brows. "Are you asking me to be one?"

"I'm trying out this list of 'first time for everything' stuff. So far, my friend pool has been limited to Court members and my aunt." I shrug. "I'm branching out."

Elias chuckles. "I'll be a first then." Nodding one final time, he enters Coffee Haven.

I hug my cup. Christmas music spills out of the shops down the street, the end of Thanksgiving a welcome reminder that jollier things are on the air. Big ribbons are tied on lampposts and lights are strung along the buildings, mostly unlit until night falls. This is my favorite time of year—the gap between the holiday spent giving thanks and the holiday spent sharing love and friendship.

This is a holiday season meant for magic . . . and maybe a little courage, too. Eggnog spiked with liquor from my aunt's collection would help, but I was never good at relying on liquid courage.

I rely on me.

Inhaling deeply, I turn and face the one place I've spent a lifetime avoiding—Shelf Indulgence. The bookstore is lit up, the inside a mixture of books and cushy furniture that invites customers to stay a while. The big showcase window is empty, a stack of decorations piled against it, and I know by the way the owner scurries back and forth beyond the glass that she has huge plans for her Christmas exhibit.

Books displayed at the front of the store glare at me, the words scrawled on their covers mocking me. Voices whisper in my head, and I clench my jaw.

Not without my permission, I growl inwardly.

"Squeeze any harder, and you're going to break your cup." Elias appears next to me, a fresh cup of coffee cradled in his hands. He's not as tall as Lucas, but he's broader. He has the frame of a bodybuilder with short, messy dark brown hair and full lips that would bring him a lot of attention if he didn't have the beard. Releasing his cup with one hand, he tugs on the brim of a baseball cap he wears pulled low, a Havenwood Falls Ski-ventures logo printed on the front. "It will get easier over time. All powers are like that."

I glance at him. "Do you know anything about what I am?"

He stares at the bookstore. "We all have demons that haunt us. You are a scary person, Harper Sinclair. You can channel darkness and attack people with their own nightmares."

My breath catches in my throat. "I don't want to do that."

"I know." He looks at me. "That's what saves you."

The way he stands—his muscular arms making him look like a bear inside his pullover, his baseball cap casting a shadow over his face—makes me smile. "I hope I don't offend you when I say I own a scary-looking baseball bat that would look right at home in your hands."

He laughs, the sound as gravelly as his voice. Rock stars would weep. Yet, the *way* he laughs sounds new, too. Maybe untried?

"You don't do that enough, do you?" I ask.

He sobers. "What?"

"Laugh like that."

He smiles softly. "Maybe I don't."

"You should."

"I'll keep that in mind."

We stare at the bookstore.

"Do I smell like Hell to you?" I ask, turning to him.

He snorts. "Is everything out of your mouth always this unexpected?"

"Do I?"

He takes a sip of his coffee, and then says, "You smell good." There's nothing flowery about his words, and I find I like that.

Turning away, he gets ready to lope across the street.

"Do you come here often?" I ask out of nowhere. "For coffee, I mean?"

He glances back at me. "I do."

"Good . . . you know, you should switch to hot chocolate. It's more holiday-ish. As a matter of fact," my gaze flicks to Coffee Haven and then back to him, "the town Hot Cocoa and Cookie Crawl will be happening soon. That's as good a time as any to switch."

"Have you ever done the Crawl before?" Elias asks, his booted feet on the curb, a knowing glint in his eyes. "Or is this on your 'first time for everything' list?"

I shrug. "Branching out, remember?"

"You need a phone, Ms. Sinclair," he calls while crossing the street.

"Maybe I'll get one," I call in return.

Smiling, I turn back to the bookstore. New friends. A possible phone. Books I might attempt to read. People I want to try to talk to.

Christmas books start to pile up in the showcase window, and I briefly catch the title of one. *A Christmas Carol.*

My lips curl. My Aunt Eloise has forced me to listen to *A Christmas*

Carol every Christmas for as far back as I can remember. First by reading it, and then in audio. It became tradition. I'm not sure why the book is her favorite, but by making me listen to it year after year, she's made it one of my favorites, too.

I suddenly feel the urge to hug Eloise. For nothing more than just being her. Now that I know my powers can be controlled, I can start building an even closer relationship with her, the kind of relationship I should have had before.

Who knows? Maybe, just maybe, I am Havenwood Falls' version of Scrooge. Only I'm not old or miserly. I'm a recluse imprisoned by fears rather than faults. My ghosts of Christmas past, present, and future are two villains, a fallen angel, and a sentient weapon.

A work truck roars to life, and I glance at the street just in time to see Elias driving off, his window rolled down. His hand lifts in a wave, and I wonder about his story.

But first . . .

Today is the first day in a new beginning.

CHAPTER 17

*N*ew beginnings mean less fear, right?

At least that's what I kept telling myself when I left Main Street for the one place I felt safe enough to practice my powers. After a hug fest with my aunt, which is less weird than it sounds, I hole myself up at her shop in a space I never even attempted to enter until now.

I am not afraid of my powers. I am not afraid of my powers. Over and over again, I repeat the mantra in my head, my eyes on the walls of the back room. The reading room, my aunt calls it.

There are notebooks and pencils everywhere. It looks like a wet dream for writers. For me, not so much.

I am not a coward.

The door to the shop dings. Customers enter, and then exit. Time ticks forward.

Eloise has a client scheduled for the afternoon, and I know by the impatient way she paces the floor beyond where I stare at the wall, that I'm running out of time.

"Hey, Eloise," a voice greets, her words chasing the door's bell. "Harper around?"

Relief and trepidation flood my veins. Addie Beaumont. Saundra's granddaughter.

The bead curtain behind me clicks together.

"Hey," Addie says gently. She walks in front of me, her studiously edgy appearance a welcome one. Light brown hair fans out over a red sweater, the shirt resting over ripped jeans. A diamond in her nose winks at me when she leans down, her eyes softening behind her glasses. "Bet you can't guess why I'm here."

"That fast, huh?"

In her arms is a leather satchel, the bag home to a tattoo kit. Adelaide Beaumont is here to mark me. All of the supernaturals in Havenwood Falls are marked when they come to town as a way to register with the Court. It keeps tabs on the supes. I'm one of them now. Always had been, I guess.

"They definitely don't take their time with things." She taps me on the arm. "Where and what?" She doesn't have to say more than that. I know how it works.

"My wrist. A quill pen."

She chuckles. "That makes sense."

Pulling a pad and pencil out of her bag, she gets to work sketching the design before tracing it with a purple pen and removing it.

Giving her my arm, I look away. Even if I was afraid of needles, the pain would be nothing compared to the pain I've already faced. To the way my heart feels now, torn between jubilation and heartbreak. New beginnings and loneliness.

Damp paper is pressed against my skin. "What you did last night was incredible," Addie tells me.

My eyes drop to the table. "Can you help me with something?"

Addie pauses. "Depends."

"I want to try to use my powers."

"Now?" she asks, startled.

"No." I shake my head, smiling. I know by the way I've stared at the wall for hours that I'm not ready. But I will be. "Not now. But soon." I look at her. "I'm going to be something big, Addie. I'm going to be a part of this town. A part of this community in a way I never was before. When I'm ready, will you come? I'd feel better if there was a witch there. You know . . . just in case."

Placing her hand against mine, she peers down at the design on my wrist, at the tattoo she's about to start on. "You've had a long, hard road, Harper. A lot of us admire what you've been through and how you've handled it. I'll be there."

As she's tattooing me, I stare at her. She's strong, too. I may not know a lot about what I can do yet, but I see and feel the strength in her.

"I want to be a part of what makes this town safe," I say suddenly.

Addie smiles. "Good. We'll both be a part of that."

Nodding, I shut my eyes. My time is coming.

CHAPTER 18

 hristmas Eve

THE WALK-IN UTILITY closet in my kitchen makes a perfect darkroom, and I outfitted it exactly the way I need it to be.

Landscape photography is a competitive business, but I've managed to make a name for myself and a decent paycheck—enough for a single woman—mainly by taking pictures no one else has been able to capture. It's easy to get unseen shots when I'm the only person snapping pictures of the mountains and landscape around Havenwood Falls for print in magazines. Most of my photographs are labeled as remote spots in Colorado with no specific name attached.

I'm careful not to snap shots of the shifters or other supernaturals that roam the hillsides. All of my photos have to be approved before I sell them, but I've been making a freelance cash flow from my work since my last year in high school.

A photographic safelight swings above my messy bun, the glow from the bulb turning the entire space red. My fingers clutch a pair of tongs, my eyes on a developing tray.

I get a thrill from this process because everything has to be perfect. From the water temperature to the exposure duration.

The picture I'm working on now is no different.

From developer to stop bath to fixer to the rinse, I take my time with it. Careful. Ever so careful.

The image that appears is exactly what I expected it to be.

"Why do you want that anyway?" Desi asks from my feet. For some reason, he's taken a real interest in my photography. Maybe sentient weapons need hobbies, too.

I stare at the picture. "Because there's nothing like framing a falling star."

Before me is a photograph of the mountain, pine trees and snow a backdrop to a walking wall of flames.

Lucas.

My falling star.

Maybe he'll be back. I certainly hope he returns, but if he doesn't, he gave me something I will never forget. He gave me confidence.

In a weird way, he also gave me purpose. He may have been the reason the archdemon Leviathan came into my life, but without the experience, I wouldn't have discovered what I am. I wouldn't have discovered what I can be.

I'd be living handicapped by words and held back by fear.

My thoughts stray to Gillian, and my stomach churns. Because of her magic, the demoness is as much my mother as my own flesh and blood mother. Two women. One evil, the other good. I am a part of both of them. One dead, the other's fate uncertain.

I'm not sure what that means for me now, but I'm willing to find out.

Hanging the picture up to dry, I exit the darkroom and pull out a new cell phone from my blue jeans pocket. Cell service may be terrible in the mountains, spotty at best on a good day, but at least I'm moving into the current century with modern technology.

Thumbing through my contacts, I click on a new name entered only recently.

Me: *Did you know that April is National Grilled Cheese Sandwich Month?*

Him: *No, I can't say I knew that.*

Me: *April twelfth is National Grilled Cheese Sandwich Day. I Googled it.*

Him: *Did you know that the term 'grilled cheese' made its first print appearance in the 1960s? I lived it.*

Me: *Overachiever.*

A few minutes pass, and then,

Him: *You're texting now?*

Me: *I'm trying.*

Those two words hold a lot of meaning. Words and I may never get along. I still feel the whispers when I try to read a book or when I try to write a word, but I'm getting better at pushing them back.

I have goals. Small ones. Each step a bigger one than the last. I started with a sentence. Next came a paragraph. Then a page. One day, I will finish a book. For now, I'll keep listening to them.

For now, I'll frame my falling star and remind myself that some wishes do come true.

EPILOGUE

N̄ew Year's Day

IT IS JUST after midnight on New Year's Day when Addie Beaumont knocks on the door of my aunt's shop. I'd stayed the night with Eloise, mainly to watch the fireworks in town from the room upstairs, a storage area full of boxes and insane clutter. Eloise is a closet hoarder.

"People should be kissing and doing, I don't know, things *other* than wanting to channel entities on New Year's," Addie complains when I open the door.

I grin. "This is my New Year's Resolution."

"What? Using your powers?" In black denim, a hoodie, and combat boots, Addie looks ready to take on the world. It makes me wonder what kind of New Year's resolutions she's made.

"To start *mastering* my powers."

"Harper's a go-getter," Aunt Eloise calls from the back of the shop. Pulling the hoodie up on her onesie unicorn pajamas, she waves at Addie before disappearing down the back basement stairs.

Addie laughs. "Only Eloise could pull that off."

"You should have seen her on Christmas." Locking the shop behind her, I lead the way to the reading room.

A small lamp is the only light in the space, and I turn it on, the dim glow casting as many shadows as it does light.

"The mortal clients must dig the dimness. It was a bitch tattooing you in this light," Addie says.

Two chairs rest at a small table, on opposite sides facing each other. I take one of them, and Addie takes the other. Paper and pencils rest on the surface between us.

She looks at me, her eyes wide behind her glasses. "You're sure about this."

"Are you?"

"Fuck it, let's do this."

Her words tug a smile out of me, and I place my hand on the table. A witch and a psychic summoner. That's what New Year's looks like in Havenwood Falls. For the two of us, anyway.

My hand starts to tremble, and I glare at it. "I want to know more about myself," I say aloud.

With a speed I don't expect, my fingers grab a pencil and move to the paper, scratching words faster than I can keep up with them. The light in the room flickers.

Darkness. Light. Darkness.

When it pops on again, shadows circle us, but these shadows aren't from the dim lighting. These are the ghosts from the ridge, the specters who held down Gillian until she was taken away.

"Holy shit!" Addie exclaims.

The shadows start to whisper, each of them edging toward me, expectant. I know if I told them to go somewhere or do something, they'd do it. Power fills me, the feeling so strong and amazing, I have to remind myself not to abuse it.

"Talk to me," I demand.

My hand continues to write. *Athame. Magic. Necromancer. Artifact. This is how you became.*

Addie leans over the paper. "Athame? The one Gillian used against you at the ridge?" Her eyes narrow. "Necromancer . . . a necromancer's athame."

Our eyes meet. The words don't flow as easily as they did on Thanksgiving, and I wonder if it's me being too cautious.

"A necromancer's athame. Life," I whisper. "She stabbed my mother with it. That would explain how it saved me."

Addie glances at the Hell ghosts. "And how you can do this. This is fucking creepy. I hope you know that, Harper."

Like her, I glance at them. "Bring us the scotch in the shop," I command.

One of the shadows departs the back room only to return seconds later, the bottle of liquor landing on the table in front of us. We both stare at it.

"Fucked up," Addie mumbles. Grabbing the bottle, she opens it, upends it, and takes a swig. "Yeah, this called for that."

My hand races back to the paper, scribbling furiously.

"Addie," I breathe.

She glances at the words, her face going white.

"Leave us," I cry.

The shadows vanish, and my pencil clatters to the table. Grabbing the scotch, I take a swig. I may not understand most of what I've written, but I know enough to realize it's not good.

"I'm sorry," I breathe. Addie takes the paper, stands, and stares down at me. She doesn't even have to say anything. I stop her before she can. "My lips are sealed."

"What you just did," she swallows hard, "it was crazy amazing, Harper. You're right. You do have incredible power."

Standing, I place a hand on her shoulder. "If you need anything . . . if I can do anything . . ."

Addie crumples the paper in her fist. "I'm going to kill that son of a bitch."

Picking up the scotch, I offer it to her. "Is that a New Year's resolution?"

"It's something," she says, upending the bottle once more before rushing to the front of the store. "Look—"

"Go," I tell her. "I understand. I just hate I'm the bearer of bad news."

"No, you're the opposite of that. You're shedding light on the truth." At the door, she gives me a small smile before slipping outside.

"Happy New Year's," I whisper, the door banging shut behind her.

For a long time I stand at the door, my eyes on the street, my hands tucked into the pockets of a navy hoodie. Pajama bottoms decorated with cameras cover my legs. My feet are stuffed into socks and unicorn slippers. The slippers are courtesy of my aunt.

A rumble rises down the street, headlights swinging as a truck pulls onto Eleventh Street, stopping in front of the shop. There's something reassuring about the man I know is driving it. He's strong in a silent, steady way that's fortifying.

The driver's side window rolls down.

My lips curve into a smile.

WE HOPE you enjoyed this story in the Havenwood Falls series of novellas featuring a variety of supernatural creatures. Keep going for an excerpt of *Lose You Not* by Kristie Cook. The series is a collaborative effort by multiple authors. Each book is generally a stand-alone, so you can read them in any order, although some authors have written sequels to their own stories. Please be aware when you choose your next read.

Havenwood Falls books by R.K. Ryals:

Ink & Fire
The Collector: Awakening
Curse the Night
Dark Seduction (with Michele G. Miller)

BOOKS YOU MIGHT ALSO ENJOY in the main Havenwood Falls series:

Forget You Not by Kristie Cook
Nowhere to Hide by Belinda Boring
Rock Me Gently by Susan Burdorf
Toil & Trouble by Melissa Wright
Of Salt and Stars by Seven Jane

Immerse yourself in the world of Havenwood Falls and stay up to date on news and announcements at www.HavenwoodFalls.com.

ABOUT THE AUTHOR

R.K. Ryals is the author of emotional and gripping young adult and new adult paranormal romance, contemporary romance, and fantasy. With a strong passion for charity and literacy, she works as a full-time writer encouraging people to "share the love of reading one book at a time." An avid animal lover and self-proclaimed coffee-holic, R.K. Ryals was born in Jackson, Mississippi, and makes her home in the Southern United States with her husband, three daughters, a playful cat named Delphi, and a coffeepot she honestly couldn't live without. Should she ever become the owner of a fire-breathing dragon (tame of course), her life would be complete. Visit her at www.authorrkryals.com.

ACKNOWLEDGMENTS

A book is a journey no one takes alone. I owe so much to the people who have followed me on this crazy adventure.

First, I have to thank my husband, whose patience and diligence in the face of my crazy coffee-induced long days should be reserved for saints. His tireless support means the world. Thanks to my daughters, who inspire me on a daily basis. I am truly blessed with amazing children. They have passion, determination, and resilience. Raising them to be the strong women I am watching them become humbles me.

A heartfelt thank you to my personal assistant, Christina Silcox. I am so very grateful for all of the late-night messages, motivating phone calls, and unerring friendship. I am proud to call you a part of my family. You amaze me.

To Jessica Johnson and Amanda Engelkes, who have spent the last two months letting me use them for a sounding board. This has been so important to me and *for* me. Thank you.

A special thank you to a group of loyal women who have followed me since the beginning of my career. To my Archive girls and my Scribes group, the dedication you have shown me is not taken for granted.

There are no words big enough to express how grateful I am to be a part of the Havenwood Falls family. Thank you, Kristie Cook, for creating this world and allowing all of us to play in it. It is no easy task to build a shared universe, and I am blown away by the hard work and diligence you put into everything you do. What an amazing and talented family you have allowed me to enter.

Huge thanks and crushing hugs to the Havenwood Falls authors who let me borrow the wonderful characters that make this story so strong. To Michele G. Miller, for the use of Elias. He is a wonderful character and was such a joy to work with. He has definitely left an impression on Harper and on me. To Kristie Cook, for the use of Saundra Beaumont. Her strength and firm loyalty to Havenwood Falls brings this novella full circle. Also for the use of Addie Beaumont. To E.J. Fechenda, for the use of Elsmed and Willow Fairchild. Having them involved in Ink & Fire brought Harper the strength and empathy she needed to move forward. To Kallie Ross, for the use of Ric Kasun. Havenwood Falls could not ask for a better sheriff. These characters lent so much to this story and to Harper's development. To the rest of the Havenwood Falls authors, for the characters they've created, some of which are mentioned in Harper's journey.

A massive shout out to Regina Wamba for the beautiful cover art. The Havenwood Falls novellas would not be the same without you. Your work astounds me.

To the Havenwood Falls family. Every day we grow bigger and stronger. A shared universe is born from the strength of its members. I respect all of you so very much. Your talent, dedication, and friendship is something I will always be grateful to know and be a part of.

To my Redemption fans who gave me the push to want to bring Lucas back to life even for a little while. He was a part of a series that birthed my career, and I can't thank all of you enough for being a part of that.

Finally, to my readers, you take my breath away. It means the world that you read my words. I am extremely grateful for your support on this insane journey full of crazy twists and turns. My love to you always.

~ A Havenwood Falls New Adult Novel ~

HAVENWOOD FALLS

LOSE YOU NOT

KRISTIE COOK

Lose You Not (A Havenwood Falls Novel) by Kristie Cook

The sequel to *Forget You Not*, this full-length novel continues the story of Michaela and Xandru—because finding someone means you can lose them again.

With her past memories mostly restored, Michaela Petran begins to pick up the pieces and resettle into life in Havenwood Falls. But resuming where she left off with the man she loves and the plans they'd made is no simple matter. Suddenly head of the family and leader of the moroi vampires, she faces an onslaught of unexpected obligations, making her feel like she has no choices in her own life. And even if she could have everything she wants, she can't help but fear it'll all be ripped away from her once again.

For five years, Xandru Roca ached for Michaela to return, but never believed it would actually happen. Now that he has a second chance with her, he's afraid he'll blow it by hanging on too tightly. But if he's not careful, she might again vanish from his life.

As they try to bridge the chasm between them, family matters demand their attention, pulling them apart. After all, there's still a strigoi curse, dictates of the supernatural Court, and dark magic wreaking havoc on their siblings. Family and love always come first, but while they try to save one, they risk losing the other.

LOSE YOU NOT

MICHAELA

"Badass vampire. I'm a badass vampire. I can do this."

Chanting the words out loud, I followed a horrendous stink down the third-floor hallway of Whisper Falls Inn, built by my father in 1854 and inherited by his twenty-four-year-old daughter, yours truly. Armored in elbow-length rubber gloves, an old hoodie, sweatpants, and shit-kicker boots, I pulled a scarf up over my nose and mouth, then held the broom upside down, ready to swing. I stopped at the end of the hall, in front of one of our two suites, this one in the uppermost turret of the Victorian mansion. Nobody had seen the guest since dusk last night, but the room key showed up on the front desk early this morning, and by noon, this odor had permeated all the way downstairs to the lobby. I had no idea what the guy had done in there, but judging by the putrid smell, it couldn't be good.

This was what my life had become.

"I swear to all, if there's a dead body in there, I'm going to be fucking pissed." I rolled my shoulders, then yelled, because I didn't know where in the building she was, "Mammie, I'm going in!"

Before I could lose my nerve, I slammed the door open and jumped back, just in case something pounced.

"Oh. My. *God!*" I screeched, bile rising into my mouth. I threw my arm across my face. "Oh god, oh god, oh god."

The only thing that pounced was the smell, a gazillion times worse now. My eyes watered, and my chest heaved as I fought the urge to puke. I tightened my grip on the broom handle and slowly made my way into the suite, my gaze sweeping the circular room. Blinking against the tears, I saw nothing out of the ordinary. The sitting area looked untouched. The bed was rumpled, obviously slept in last night —before the jerk took off without checking out—but nothing gross stained the bedding, despite the stench. Like feces. Or vomit. Or other bodily fluids.

The odor wafted strongest from the bathroom. Of course. I gave myself another pep talk as I inched my way there, which gave Madame Luiza, aka Mammie, plenty of time to find me and glide into the room.

"Oh, dear," she said. And considering she was a ghost, if she could smell it, it was bad. "Be careful, Michaela."

With her Romanian accent, my aunt said my name with its original pronunciation—Me-*hay*-la—rather than with the hard *k* everyone else gave it. Of course, everyone else tended to give me a nickname: Kaela, Kales, even Kaekae.

Because that was totally badass.

"How bad can it be?" I squared my shoulders and lifted my chin.

"I'll go in first," Mammie said. "Nothing can make me deader than I already am."

Before I could protest, she disappeared into the bathroom and returned only a heartbeat later. If ghosts could be green, she would have been. Her purple ball gown, in which she was perpetually dressed, appeared to be no worse for the wear, but that didn't really mean much, considering. Her cheeks puffed out, as though she fought a gag, and she clamped her hands over her mouth. She couldn't actually puke, but with that kind of reaction, whatever that bathroom harbored was way worse than I thought.

"Badass vampire," I repeated in a firm whisper before forcing myself through the bathroom doorway. And then I froze, staring at the scene in front of me. "What the fuck?"

"Language, dear," Mammie admonished, her voice muffled behind her hands.

"Really, Mammie? There's absolutely nothing else to say!"

A pinkish gelatinous goo stuck to nearly every surface, as though a giant troll had sneezed, spraying pink snot everywhere. It was splattered all over the faded and stained wallpaper, clung to the chipped porcelain sink and old-fashioned tub, and slid slimy trails down the warped mirror. Something large and plasma-y filled the toilet, pouring over the edge and slopping onto the yellowed tile floor.

I spun the broom and jabbed at it with the stick end. It shook like jelly. I lifted it with the broom handle, and my stomach lurched.

"He *molted*?" I shrieked. "That son of a bitch *molted* in my inn? And what the hell molts like *this*?"

The substance was not at all like a reptile skin. Not papery and dry. More like a big, bloodless placenta.

But mammals didn't molt.

"Skinwalker," Mammie whispered. "It must be. I *knew* he was no regular shifter."

"Skinwalker?" I echoed.

"They shed their skin to take on another—a whole different appearance. Sometimes a whole different life. They're very rare. I've only ever met one before, back in the 1920s."

"So what's all over the walls and everything else? Do these skinwalkers explode, too?"

Mammie patted her silver bun as she glanced around, then shrugged. "Maybe if their new body is larger than their old skin?"

"Ew! Gross." I shuddered at the image while trying to hold back the vomit that kept making its way up the back of my throat.

Groaning, I poked and prodded the gunk, working it out of the toilet, because it obviously was not going to flush through the pipes. Finally, the end of it flopped out of the bowl and onto the floor, splashing at my feet and sending Mammie out into the bedroom part of the suite. I tried pushing it out of the way with the broom handle. At first it jiggled, but barely moved. So I gave it a harder shove, and the handle slipped right through the substance like a knife through warm butter and drove into the wall. Little black things—and some not so little—poured out of the hole and scurried over the wall.

"Ahhhhh!"

I ran out of the bathroom screaming, with Mammie right on my heels, shrieking even louder. We flew through the hall, down the steps, rounding the flights, not stopping until we hit the lobby three floors down. I fell to my knees, panting and heaving, my whole body trembling as my hands pressed into my chest, as if they could slow my heart.

"Spiders," I choked out. "Fucking spiders."

Mammie burst out laughing.

Lifting my head, I glared at her with narrowed eyes.

She tried to rein herself in. "I'm sorry, dear. If you could have only seen your face. Are you sure you're moroi?"

"Hey!" I waggled a finger at her. "You were running and screaming, too."

"I was not running," she denied, but a smile twitched at her lips. "I can't run, dear. Ghosts fly."

And for some reason, that statement broke through my fear, and laughter consumed me until I was crying. Once I was able to compose myself, I pushed up to my feet.

"We're burning the whole place down," I declared as the front door opened.

A teen and a tween, both dark-haired, entered, the smell of an early summer evening carried in with them—pine, freshly mown grass, and wildflowers.

"You're *what?*" Gabe, my twelve-year-old brother, asked, his eyes wide in his thin face. They were still brown because he was still human, meaning his moroi gene hadn't been triggered. That usually happened at around twenty years old.

"Gabe decided he didn't want to hang out with Cody after all, so I brought him home," Aurelia, our sixteen-year-old sister, also still human, whined as she followed behind him, both of their slender bodies clad in shorts and tanks.

What they called summer here in the mountains was a lot closer to the winters I'd grown used to during my five years in Atlanta. So while everyone else already wore summer attire, I was still comfortable in hoodies and jeans. And technically, summer didn't start until next week. Maybe by the end of July, I'd dare a pair of shorts.

"He could have walked," Aurelia continued. "It's not like it's all that far, but noooo, whiny baby insisted on a ride. Oh, well. Lena didn't want to do anything, and Laurel was being a snot anyway." Her nose wrinkled as she finally got over herself and noticed her surroundings. "What died?" Her eyes flew wide open, and she had the decency to throw a hand over her mouth in embarrassment as she looked at Mammie. "I didn't . . . I mean . . . what stinks?"

"Spiders. And gross stuff. You don't want to know," I answered.

"Spiders?" she and Gabe said at the same time. Except Aurelia sounded as freaked out as I was, while excitement colored Gabe's tone.

"Hey, don't you have a hot date tonight?" Aurelia asked me as her chocolate eyes gave me a once-over, her nose scrunching even more.

"As a matter of fact, I do," said a deep voice, preceding its owner from the front vestibule.

His tall, muscular frame emerged into the lobby, clothed in a dress shirt and black pants, rather than his usual T-shirt and jeans. The lavender color of his shirt, along with his dark hair and beard stubble, brought out the brightness of his gray-green eyes—the eyes that always got me. The eyes that had been the one aspect of Havenwood Falls I'd never been able to forget, even when the Luna Coven witches magically wiped my memory and replaced it with a false past. Something deep inside hadn't allowed me to completely forget Xandru Roca.

Like always, my heart went all trippy and my breath caught when I saw him.

The look he gave me in return was not quite as enamored. I glanced down at myself.

Oh, shit. "Is it that time already?"

"Rough day?" he asked.

"You could say that." I glanced upward, as though I could see through two floors to the third one. "We have a problem."

He gave me a small smile. "You go get cleaned up. I'll check it out."

"No, don't. You're all dressed up. You really don't want to deal with that." I turned to my brother. "Gabe, since you skipped out on your chores this morning, you get to take care of room 313. It's totally your kind of thing."

As I headed through the large dining room for one of the several pairs of French doors in the back, I heard footsteps ascending the grand staircase off the lobby—two pairs, one much heavier than the other—and Xandru saying, "No worries. I got your back."

Well, at least we'd both stink on our date tonight.

The sky was just beginning to darken as I strode across the rear lawn of the inn to the two-bedroom cottage the kids and I shared until we figured out . . . well, until we figured out life. We'd all been through a lot in the last several years and still weren't sure about our new normal.

Three months ago, I'd been tending bar at a club in downtown Atlanta and serving breakfast to drunks in the middle of the night, thinking I was some mutant form of vampire with a depressing past and no family. My true memories of growing up in Havenwood Falls, Colorado, population five thousand-ish, with a family who loved me and friends who still did, had mostly returned by now, although I still experienced some blank moments. But they were still just memories, not the life I'd stepped into when I came back. This new life was . . . I didn't know what it was yet.

Like I said, we were still figuring it all out.

Like what we wanted to do with the family estate. The mansion in Havenwood Heights provided a lot more space than the cottage at the inn, but without Mom, Dad, and Mammie, we all agreed it felt like *too much* room. Yet, at the same time, the memories there of when our family was whole made the walls feel like they closed in on us. I couldn't be there for more than an hour before the emotions became too much to bear—mostly sadness, but also a lot of anger.

Maybe not facing it all was a form of denial, but we chose to cram into the small cottage, the largest of the five that lined the back of the inn's property.

When they were even there, Aurelia usually slept in my bed and Gabe in the smaller bedroom, but they often took a room in the main house with Mammie to watch over them or spent the night with friends. Because of the nightmares, I tried not to sleep much at all, but when I did, it was rarely at night. The tattoo I received as my registry with the Court of the Sun and the Moon, a requirement for all supernaturals in Havenwood Falls, was infused with magic that allowed me to be outside in the sun, but after the novelty wore off, my biological clock reverted to my vampire ways. I favored the late afternoons and nights. I'd always been a night owl anyway, even before I'd been turned. So the arrangement was working for us. Sort of.

Considering everything, I felt like we were managing life quite well.

Just as I pushed the cottage's front door open, a loud splintering of wood followed by a scream came from behind me. I spun around just in time to see two bodies falling from a hole in the third-story turret and crashing through the glass ceiling of the conservatory just below it.

Screaming, I sprinted across the lawn and tried to open the outside door to the conservatory, but it was jammed. Much of the large, glass room's framework was made of copper piping, which they pumped steam through back in the day to heat the space, along with other metals for the fancy scroll work on the trim. Patina and tarnish had started to cover the metal, and rust had eaten some of it away, causing places to bend and deform, including around the door. Focusing my mind on the metal, I bent it out of the way, allowing the door to swing open. When Xandru's brother Tase had triggered my moroi gene by giving me his blood, he'd passed on to me the Rocas' ability to control metal. It came in handy sometimes.

"Are you okay?" Xandru's voice came from the shadows.

I followed the sound, weaving around boxes, junk, and covered furniture stored in the conservatory to find him setting my little brother on his feet. They both stood in a broken hole in the wooden floor, next to a full-size replica of a knight holding his sword pointy end up— they'd missed it by mere inches.

"Yeah, I think so," Gabe said, his voice shaky.

"You're bleeding!" Pulling my hoodie off, I hurried over to him and pressed it to the gash in his head.

"Is everyone okay?" Aurelia asked from the doorway to the inn.

"Call an ambulance," I ordered.

"I said I'm okay," Gabe argued.

"You have blood gushing from your head!"

Unfortunately, neither Xandru nor I could give him our blood to heal him. Because we were both mature (turned) moroi, doing so would trigger Gabe's gene, and he was way too young for that. Thankfully, his blood didn't incite any kind of thirst from Xandru or me. We had control over that part of us. Now, if Tase were here, it might have been a whole different story—he'd cursed himself to excruciating bloodlust when he triggered my gene.

If I had any say, though, Atanase "Tase" Roca would never be around my brother or sister.

"It doesn't hurt." Gabe shrugged. "Xandru caught me. It was really cool! I can't wait until I'm turned."

I visually inspected the rest of his small-for-his-age body, but only found a couple of scratches. "I'd rather be safe than sorry." I looked up at Xandru to find his pants and shirt splattered with wet marks. "Are *you* okay?"

He shook his arms, pink gunk flying off his sleeve. "Besides whatever the hell this is? Yeah, I'm fine. I always land on my feet."

I ignored his cocky grin and grabbed Gabe by the shoulders,

walking him over to sit on the step that led inside to the inn. "What happened?"

He held his fist up and opened it to reveal a beaded bracelet. "I was trying to get this. It was inside the wall you put a hole in upstairs. But the wall broke more, and the next thing I knew, I was falling through it and down to the ground. Then Xandru was there, catching me right before we hit the ground. He's right. We landed on our feet!" He looked over at the hole in the floor. "Sort of."

"I hate to say it, Ms. Petran, but your inn needs some repairs," Xandru said, as he inspected what were obviously rotted floorboards.

"You think?" I squatted next to Gabe, re-inspecting him even as he pulled away. He was more interested in his newly found treasure than any injury.

He held the bracelet up in the waning light. "Do you think it's valuable?"

"Not as valuable as your life," I muttered.

A few moments later, the ambulance arrived. An EMT named Jordan took Gabe inside the truck to clean him up and do an evaluation. The wound wasn't nearly as bad as I'd thought it was.

"Heads bleed a lot," Jordan explained as he hopped off the end of the ambulance. My vampire senses picked up on his scent with a tinge similar to Mike McCabe's—mountain lion shifter. Mike was the local building contractor and had fixed the inn's roof last month. I supposed I'd need to call him again. "He should be fine. He's not showing any signs of a concussion, but it wouldn't be a bad idea to keep an eye on him throughout the night and tomorrow."

"Oh, thank god." I blew out a sigh of relief.

Gabe was fine. Thanks to Xandru. But what if he hadn't been there to catch him? What if it had been worse? This inn was a danger zone. Worse than I had believed.

Not long after the ambulance left, another visitor arrived.

"I called the Court," Xandru explained, wiping at a spot on his shirt. "So they could get a sample of this. Mammie told me it's from a skinwalker, but I'm sure they'll want to know more."

"I know *I* want to know more. Too bad it's not Addie," I said before we walked in to greet the male witch the Luna Coven had sent. "She would tell me everything."

The Luna Coven did all of the Court of the Sun and the Moon's magical bidding. At least, that's what many of the supes in town believed. Mammie, who'd sat on the Court for a short time, had let it slip once that there were some tasks the Luna Coven couldn't dirty their hands with. Not when their High Council leaders also sat on the Court, which ruled the supernaturals in Havenwood Falls, protecting the humans and our secret. The more unappealing tasks were passed on to other, lesser covens in town.

The middle-aged man was thorough in his inspection and collection of goo, which he stored in vials and dropped into his satchel, asking me questions I mostly didn't have answers for. I didn't think it possible for him to move any slower, but at least when he was done, he helped Xandru patch the hole in the turret with a flick of his wrist and a few chanted words.

"We'll test the samples and see what we can find out about this mystery person," he said as we finally headed back downstairs. "If anything, maybe there are traces of Adelaide's ink, which she can use to identify them. You all have a good evening now."

Yeah, right. I looked outside at the dark streets, and then at Xandru, and frowned.

"It must be past midnight if the twinkle lights in the square are off."

He pulled his phone out of his pants pocket. "Twelve-oh-four, to be exact."

"Another date ruined," I murmured as I scratched at a patch of dried skinwalker gunk on the back of my hand. I really needed a shower. We both did. "I'm so very sorry."

Giving me a smile, he shrugged. "Well, at least we were able to spend some time together, even if it wasn't the perfect date."

"Do you think we'll ever have a real second date?"

He stepped in front of me and brushed his thumb over my cheek. "That I promise you, Michaela Petran." He leaned down and brushed his full lips over mine. "But we don't have to call it a night yet . . ."

His mouth lingered on mine in a luscious kiss that I eventually had to pull away from before I collapsed from a lack of oxygen.

"I'm gross," I reminded him, taking a step back.

He moved forward, closing the space I'd just put between us. "Me, too. We could clean up together."

"Hmm . . . that is tempting."

His fingers skimmed over my cheek and down my neck, producing a shiver. "But? I hear a but coming."

"But Gabe is in the cottage. There's no privacy."

His hand cupped my chin, and I could tell by the look in his eyes that he was thinking what I was—there were plenty of other places we could have gone. Upstairs, in a guest room, for instance, since we had several vacancies. Or any of the other open cottages. But he didn't say it, and neither did I. We hadn't reached that place yet.

I'd begun to wonder if we ever would.

Instead, he kissed my forehead. "Try again tomorrow?"

I gave him a smile, which I didn't quite feel on the inside. "Yeah. Sure. Tomorrow."

But tomorrow didn't come. At least, not in that sense.

As had been the case for the last three months, every day brought new obstacles that kept us from having a real date . . . or any kind of relationship at all.

Purchase *Lose You Not* at your favorite book retailer.

www.ingramcontent.com/pod-product-compliance
Lightning Source LLC
Chambersburg PA
CBHW051957170626
46808CB00007B/2665